RAVEN'S LONGEST NIGHT

By Donald MacKenzie

Donald MacKenzie

Raven's Longest Night

PUBLISHED FOR THE CRIME CLUB
BY
Doubleday & Company, Inc.
Garden City, New York
1983

All of the characters in this book are fictitious,
and any resemblance to actual persons,
living or dead,
is purely coincidental.

Library of Congress Cataloging in Publication Data

MacKenzie, Donald, 1908–
Raven's Longest Night.

I. Title.
PR6063.A243R3   1983   813'.54
ISBN: 0-385-19102-2
Library of Congress Catalog Card Number 83-11493

First Edition in the United States of America

For Jamie and Catherine Neidpath

RAVEN'S LONGEST NIGHT

CHAPTER 1

The Café Alemán was on the Paseo Santa Teresa, close to the Atocha Railway Station. It was a neighbourhood of cheap hotels and rooming-houses patronized for the most part by transients. It was six o'clock in the evening and the bars were already crowded. The interior of the Café Alemán was decorated with green-and-blue tiles depicting dolphins and mermaids. Lobsters crawled sluggishly across the bottoms of salt-water tanks. White-aproned waiters shuffled through the sawdust juggling trays loaded with chilled beer, crabs, clams and goose-barnacles.

The restaurant encroached on the pavement, where a faded orange awning shielded four tables from the sun. The wet checked cloths were pinned to the tables each morning and allowed to dry. A strong reek of ammonia drifted from the nearby alley-way.

Stephen Szechenyi was sitting at one of these outside tables drinking his first brandy of the day. He was seventy years old and bald except for an outbreak of straggly white hair fringing his ears. His slate-coloured eyes were set narrowly over a nose like a falcon's beak. He was in his customary chair, dressed in a seersucker suit bought in the bargain basement of the Corte Inglés. Its colour had once been light grey. By moving slightly, he could see his office windows in the dingy building across the street. He used the café as a sort of club, reading his newspaper there and playing the occasional game of chess, indifferent to the noise and fumes of the passing traffic.

He turned now, startled to hear himself greeted in his native Hungarian by a total stranger. The newcomer took the free chair and removed his panama hat, continuing to speak in Hungarian.

"You will forgive the intrusion, Count Szechenyi. My name is Gotsek, Nicholas Gotsek."

He slid a visiting-card across the table. It bore no address or telephone number, nothing but the name. He was a healthy-looking man in his forties, dressed in a blue flannel suit and a white silk shirt. His hair and eyebrows were a light shade of rust. He offered a package of English cigarettes, smiling encouragingly.

Szechenyi shook his head. "I do not smoke."

Gotsek ordered a coffee from the hovering waiter. "You are probably right. I wish I could give it up." He paused to use an expensive gold lighter, his eyes half-closed as he glanced across the table. "You are a long way from home."

"This *is* my home," Szechenyi said, frowning.

Gotsek waved his cigarette, holding it between thumb and index finger. "Of course, in the sense that you have lived here, brought up a family here, and so forth. I am referring to your real home, your spiritual home."

Szechenyi summoned what remained of his presence and started to rise to his feet.

"Don't go," Gotsek said quickly. "Let me assure you that it is in your interest to hear me out."

Szechenyi sat down again. "Who are you? What do you want from me?"

Gotsek made himself comfortable in his chair. "What we want, Count Szechenyi, is your co-operation. I understand your distress, but you must have known that this meeting was inevitable."

Szechenyi found the ground with his feet and braced himself. There had always been the hope at the back of his mind that they would accept defeat and forget him.

Gotsek appeared to read his thoughts. "Of course, we have always known where you were. In fact, your name was one of the first that I heard when I joined the ministry. You would be surprised at the amount of paperwork you have occasioned over the years." There was a touch of wry humour about his smile.

Szechenyi's fingers closed round his empty glass. Gotsek signalled for a refill.

"You're wasting your time," said Szechenyi. "The courts have made their decision."

"The courts!" Gotsek put his head on one side. "This money is not rightfully yours and you know it full well."

"The money belongs to Hungary," Szechenyi said doggedly.

"Bravo!" Gotsek smiled approvingly. "At least we are agreed on the basic issue!" Gotsek weighed his lighter in the palm of his hand. "You're an educated man. You know how it is. Rulers come and go but the country remains. We are both patriots, each in his own way."

Szechenyi's face was stony. "You're forgetting something. I have seen your kind of patriot in action."

Gotsek's expression sobered. "That was a terrible thing to have happened and you have my deepest sympathy. But let me assure you, things have changed at home, changed for the better. The days of Kádár have gone. Do I look like a murderer, for instance?"

Szechenyi's eyes shifted unwillingly. "You look what you are. The clothes alter nothing."

Gotsek leaned forward, his manner confidential. "You do me an injustice, Count Szechenyi. I abhor violence. You are out of touch with reality. There is no repression at home. Our country is the most liberal in Eastern Europe. Why don't you come and see for yourself?"

The raw alcohol had fired Szechenyi's courage. "Not even in a coffin! The Russians may have gone, but as far as I am concerned, Hungary is still an occupied country. Only the uniforms have changed."

"That's balderdash," Gotsek said impatiently. "Listen to

what I am saying. You have already done more than your duty, and the old ways have gone for ever. There is no flame to pass on, nobody to receive it. Anything else is just wishful thinking. Be sensible! The slate can still be wiped clean. Why not enjoy what is left of your life?"

A shoeshine boy swooped. Szechenyi waved him away. "I do not like your manner," he said pugnaciously. "I warn you that I am known here!"

Gotsek clicked his tongue against the roof of his mouth. "Don't be ridiculous. Look, I come here in friendship. The truth of the matter is that you have become a source of major embarrassment. Not only has a fortune been wasted in legal fees, but you have succeeded in making us a laughing-stock. However, make no mistake about it, you will not be allowed to enjoy this money."

Szechenyi raised his head, chicken-necked but proud. "I never wanted to enjoy it. I am no more than a custodian."

Gotsek's manner changed abruptly. "*Custodian?*" he repeated. "I will tell you what you are, Count Szechenyi. You are a thief, an old man who has been living like a dog for a generation and more! A drunkard with a neurotic daughter and a son who spends his time chasing women. You can spare me the lofty sentiments, my friend, I know you too well!"

Szechenyi's hands were shaking and he found it difficult to speak. "I've told you what we want," said Gotsek, persuasive again. "Keep half a million and drop all claim to the rest of the money. Half a million dollars," he repeated.

A perverse wish to know the worst impelled Szechenyi's next question. "And if I don't agree to co-operate, as you call it?"

Gotsek's voice acquired an edge again. "You're obliging me to say things that were better left unsaid. You're going to have to come to heel, one way or another. If my mission fails, others will take over, and I warn you that their approach will be very different from mine."

The strength had drained from Szechenyi's body, but he managed a show of defiance.

"I am not afraid to die, if that's what you mean."

"Die?" Gotsek bubbled a laugh. "Let me make one thing very clear, Count Szechenyi. Your life is of no interest to us, but you do have two children."

A cold hand clutched at Szechenyi's throat. "You're bluffing."

"Try me," said Gotsek, still smiling. "I don't bluff. We could have unloaded you at any moment we liked, and you know it! This is a genuine offer, my friend, and I urge you to take it seriously. It's the best thing for both of us. In a sense, we are allies." He arranged some coins on the top of his cheque.

"I need time," Szechenyi said with an effort. "There are things to consider. I must have time to think."

"Of course you need time," Gotsek said quickly. He reached inside his jacket and placed an envelope on the table in front of Szechenyi. "Open it!"

The blank transfer-form inside was issued by the Banque Suisse et Ottomane in Geneva. Gotsek offered a look of encouragement.

"All it needs is the number of the account and your signature, a simple procedure that will solve all our problems. You keep half a million and the rest is transferred to us. Don't worry about the details. We'll let you know later. You're going to Lisbon tomorrow. When are you coming back?"

Szechenyi passed a hand over his wet forehead, stunned by the other man's knowledge of his movements.

"I'm not sure yet."

"No problem," said Gotsek, pocketing his lighter and cigarettes. "You know, I'm always a little envious of these family reunions. I'm an orphan myself. Talk things over with your children. I'm confident that you will reach the right decision. I'll be in touch in a couple of days, one way or another. So, goodbye, Count Szechenyi." He rose, making a courteous inclination of the head, and was gone in a matter of seconds, lost in the crowd of late-evening shoppers.

Szechenyi walked into the restaurant and drank two brandies at the bar in rapid succession. Then he made his way to the Metro station. He surfaced at the Florida stop, clinging to the escalator rail. The scene was familiar: the grey-uniformed policeman, lolling against the wall, sinister in wraparound sunglasses; the blind lottery-ticket vendor, intoning his numbers from a stool near the booking-office. There was no breeze to temper the oppressive heat outside. This was the main highway to Burgos. Giant trucks thundered north, rattling the windows of the newly constructed office-blocks. Cranes towered against a backdrop of partially built factories.

Szechenyi took the short-cut home. A small park sloped down to covered walkways connecting terracotta-coloured tower blocks with a communal center and laundry. The buildings had the charm of a high-security prison. He walked a little unsteadily, avoiding the flying Frisbees and the charging bodies of children. Sun and oil-fumes had seared the grass and the trees that attempted to grow. He left the park through a gate at the foot of the hill and opened the iron door at the end of one of the walkways.

The walls and ceiling were dank with condensation. Lights burned here all year round. He emerged into a lobby with peeling murals and vast dirty windows. The elevator took him up to the ninth floor, and he let himself into his apartment. Safe in the tiny hallway, he pressed his ear against the front door. All he heard was the noise of his neighbour's radio. He hurried into the kitchen and stationed himself at the window, looking down at the deserted car-park. He shrugged and let the curtain fall. There was no need to follow him. They already knew where he lived and where he was going.

He poured himself a shot from the bottle of cheap brandy

on the shelf behind, topped up the glass with water, and took it into his bedroom. More than half his life had been passed in this apartment. At the beginning it was supposed to have been no more than a temporary resting-place, somewhere to stay while he struggled to master his father-in-law's stamp-dealing business. As it turned out, Maria-Dolores had borne their two children in the same bed in which she died twenty-four years later, surrounded by the same shoddy furniture. Life had never been easy for them in Spain. In spite of Szechenyi's background, there had been no favours from Franco other than political refuge at first. It had taken six years before Szechenyi received his citizenship papers. He and his wife had lived penuriously, apart from the world that surrounded them, saving whatever money there was for their children's education.

He looked at his watch. It was a quarter to eight. Karolyi had promised to be home early. They were taking the ten o'clock flight to Lisbon in the morning. The bed creaked as he came to his feet and unlocked a cupboard. He tipped the contents of a cardboard box onto the floor—a bundle of letters bearing Swiss stamps, a green diplomatic passport, and a birth certificate. He opened the passport and looked at a picture of himself taken forty years before and wearing the uniform of a colonel in the Royal Hungarian Air Force. He put the papers in the canvas flight bag he used for travelling and kicked the empty box under the bed. The time had come for sharing a secret that he had kept for too long.

CHAPTER 2

The villa was constructed of golden-grained stone, a ranch-style building with a red-tiled roof and French windows opening onto the flagged patio. There was a small pond in the middle of the patio. Goldfish nuzzled among the weeds. A vine had been trained as a shelter. Beyond a low stone wall at the end of the patio, flower-bright dunes descended to the beach. Two rocky headlands made the crescent of sand inaccessible except by way of the villa. The clearing had been hacked out of a hundred acres of umbrella pines. A track ran through the pines, connecting with a hardtop road that in turn connected with the highway to Sintra.

It was late afternoon, but the sun was still hot, laying ice-blue shadows across the flagstones. Kirstie Raven was lying on the swing, her husband on the recliner. They had more or less lived on the beach for the last three weeks, picnicking on cheese and fruit, reading and drifting on the canvas raft. Sun and sea had burnished their bodies the colour of chestnuts. Kirstie was on her stomach, her long legs jointed back and crossed at the ankles. Apart from a cotton scarf protecting her cornsilk hair, she was naked like Raven.

"Are you listening to what I'm saying?" she demanded.

"Oh, I'm listening," he said, opening his eyes. " 'Next time I get married it certainly won't be in Toronto.' That's what you said."

"That was five minutes ago," she retorted. "I was asking what you thought of Ilona's father."

He reached for the glass of juice by his side.

"I heard that too," he said, putting the glass down again.

"Then why don't you answer?"

She worried her questions like a dog does a bone, he thought. Surf boomed in the caves below, caves plastered with sheets of mosquitoes that rarely seemed to emerge. The water exploded like smashed emeralds in the sunshine. The incoming tide had erased their footsteps from the coarse white sand.

"I'm not so sure that I *can* answer," he said, looking at her through half-closed eyes. "I haven't formed much of an opinion."

She made a sound of disgust, hitching herself up on an elbow. Beads of sweat had gathered in the fine bleached hairs at the base of her spine. "Why not?" she asked. "Most of the time you seem to make up your mind about people as they come through the door."

He raised a hand in token surrender. "I'm not too sure I want to get into this," he said mildly.

"You're copping out, is that it?"

"I am not copping out," he replied. "I'm just being cautious. You're pretty touchy about your friends."

"That's great, coming from you!" She sat up, the three gold hoops that formed her wedding-ring flashing as she touched the hair at the nape of her neck. "I was expecting that bolt of insight you're usually so free with."

He looked at her fondly. At thirty-two she had the body of a woman ten years younger.

"You mean you *really* want to know what I think?"

"You'll tell me in any case," she replied, smearing grease on her nose. "I know the signs."

"Well, for one thing, he drinks too much," he said. She continued to grease her face. "Do pray continue!"

"I wouldn't mind the drinking if he had something to say that was interesting. As it is, our conversations are limited."

He tossed her the cigarette she wanted and gave her a light. Her reward was to blow the smoke-ring he could never quite master.

"Maybe that's because he finds you difficult to talk to. People do tend to get the message when you're bored."

The criticism took him totally by surprise. "Don't be ridiculous, Kirstie," he said. "I'm able to talk to anyone and well you know it. It was part of my training, for crissakes! But there has to be dialogue. It must go two ways. According to you, Szechenyi's led an eventful life. Air attaché in Madrid during the war, before that one of Admiral Horthy's adjutants. But mention any of that and the man dries up completely. There isn't much left. I'm not too good on postage stamps."

Kirstie's voice tightened considerably. "Do you not think it's possible that Stephen Szechenyi doesn't find his past as fascinating as you seem to?"

"You asked for an opinion," he said, slapping a fly from his ear.

"Tell me something," she said, hugging her knees. "Do you like talking about Kathy?"

"Kathy?" The scar had long healed but the shot located the wound. "What's Kathy got to do with it? I call that remark in total bad taste."

"Of course," she retorted. "But it's in no worse taste than your own remark. Kathy committed suicide, right?"

He nodded guardedly, the memory indelible.

"But you don't like to talk to anyone about it, not even me. Have you any idea how Stephen's family died?"

He lifted a shoulder. "None at all. How would I?"

"Well, I'll tell you," she said. "He was in Spain when the communists invaded Hungary. His fifteen-year-old sister was raped by Russian soldiers in front of his mother and father. They killed all three of them. Do you find it strange to understand that he doesn't like to talk about that period of his life?"

"Why don't we just drop the subject?" he suggested. "You're building this up into an argument."

"And you're getting red in the face," she retorted, squinting over a smile.

He wrapped a towel round his middle. There was something ludicrous about arguing while you were naked.

"And I'll tell you something else about your friend. That guy's heading for a nervous breakdown and it isn't only the drink."

She rounded her mouth in mock admiration. "Now we have it! The trained eye sees to the heart of the matter. How about Karolyi. What's wrong with him?"

He was determined to give just as good as he got. "He's easy. He's a straight-A shit who can't keep his hands off other men's women. If we hadn't been where we were, I'd have broken his jaw for him last night."

"I'm glad you didn't try," she said calmly. "He's very light on his feet. Talking about which, I don't have to ask how you feel about Ilona."

He grinned. "Here comes the bottom line! Let me ask you something, sweetheart. Who do you really want to talk about, Szechenyi or his daughter?"

She untied the cotton scarf and shook her hair free. "Both of them."

His lack of understanding was deliberate. "Ilona wants to know what we think about her father, is that it?"

"It's not what *I* think," she retorted. "I've known him for fifteen years, but you happen to be my husband and I'm the only friend she has."

He wiped the sweat from his neck with the towel. "Tell her I think he's enormous. I'll try to live up to it."

"You can tell her yourself," she said sharply. "There'll be plenty of time while I'm in London. How are your legs, by the way?"

"My legs?" He inspected his calves. The skin was brown and smooth. It was a year since his veins had been injected. "They seem to be holding up. Why?"

"I'm amazed, after all that leaping around last night."

They had played the radio after supper, dancing on the patio. Karolyi had partnered Kirstie, his sister Raven. Szechenyi had gone to bed drunk.

"Who would ever have thought it!" Raven exclaimed. "My wife is actually jealous! Well, let me remind you of something, Ilona's your friend."

"I hadn't forgotten," she said grimly. "And I've been living with you long enough to know when you're trying to make an impression. Ilona doesn't realize how privileged she is. I'll say this much for you, darling, your dancing style may be dated, but you certainly give it all that you've got."

"I don't believe this," he said, shaking his head. "You're not being serious, are you?"

"I'm serious," she answered. "And I happen to know exactly what I'm doing."

He moved his head from side to side. "I thought Ilona and you were tight."

"That changes nothing," she said.

"It doesn't sound like it. How about those stories you tell about school, the Vestal Virgins of Vevey and so forth? All those hockey players from the Institut Selig? I thought you used to share your boy-friends."

She threw her cigarette at the sand. "That was a long time ago. I gave it up along with a lot of other things I used to do at school. At the moment I'm a one-man woman."

"Thank God for that," he said fervently. "Have we finished our workout for the day?"

"If you'll promise me something." She poked a finger in his direction.

"My life, if necessary," he said, placing his hand on his heart.

"You don't have to go to extremes." She dragged a foot across the flagstones and looked at him. "All I'm asking you to do is remember that Ilona's vulnerable."

"Oh, but I will!" he said. "I realize my power over women, but this one is safe, I swear it!"

"You better had," she retorted. "You just better had!"

He swung his feet to the ground and managed a couple of shaky knee-bends. "One last swim before they get back!"

They raced down the dunes, the hot sand burning the soles of their feet. Raven knifed through the swelling surf to the whitecaps beyond and turned on his back. Kirstie was floating a few feet away. Life had been good to him, he decided. He was forty-two years old, had no problems and a woman who loved him. He changed the wording hurriedly with a tip of his hat to the Fate Sisters. What he actually had was a woman he loved.

The stuttering sound of the Volkswagen carried across the water. He shook the salt out of his eyes and struck out for shore. Kirstie beat him by yards, employing the crawl that he had never been able to manage. The Szechenyis were crossing the patio. Raven helped Kirstie into her towelling-robe. By the time he had dried himself, Ilona and her father and brother were coming through the French windows carrying a tray with a jug of *sangria*. Ilona was handsome rather than pretty, with burnished black hair that reached to her shoulders. Her mother's Spanish blood had softened the Magyar features, but her nose and her mouth were her father's. She was wearing a red-and-white striped dress and espadrilles. Her brother had the same face as his father, narrow through the eyes with high cheekbones. His dark hair was cut to cover his ears. He was wearing slacks and a flower-patterned shirt.

Szechenyi took Raven's place on the recliner. Raven filled a couple of glasses from the jug and gave one to Kirstie.

"How was Lisbon?" he asked politely.

Szechenyi had his own drink, brandy and water in a large glass. "It was dirty and it was undisciplined." Like his son, his English was excellent, while Ilona's years in London had left her accent close to perfection.

Karolyi smiled like a man who is accustomed to being noticed. "If you listen to my father, nothing has been the same since Salazar died!" The response he plainly counted upon was not forthcoming.

Raven finished his drink. He had no particular liking for *sangria*, but at least it was cold. He smiled at Ilona, aware that Kirstie was watching him.

"No newspapers?" The English papers were usually on sale in the city.

"They hadn't arrived." She had a low-pitched voice that she used to effect. "I think I'll get on with the supper."

"I'll help you," Kirstie said quickly, gathering her beach-bag.

Karolyi followed them into the house. The sun was setting, leaving colour and form strangely clear in the fading light. The thermometer nailed to the vine gave a reading of seventy-eight degrees. Raven filled up his glass. He smiled at Szechenyi, realizing that the tête-à-tête had been contrived. He made what he hoped was the right move.

"I'm not quite sure how to say this," he ventured. "Kirstie was telling me about the terrible thing that happened to your family. I'm very sorry."

It was clearly the wrong remark. Szechenyi ignored it, staring into space. What should have been the whites of his eyes were a muddy shade of yellow.

"My son is sometimes indiscreet," he said after a while. "I hope that his remark about Salazar didn't offend you."

Raven shook his head. "On the contrary. There's a lot of truth in what you say. I knew Portugal twenty years ago. A woman could walk on the streets unmolested at three o'clock in the morning. Not any more. Read the newspapers."

Szechenyi ignored this too. "What do you believe in, Mr. Raven? Are you a religious man?"

"My friends who are wouldn't say so," said Raven. "No, I don't suppose that I am, not in the accepted sense, at any rate. I do have beliefs of a religious kind but I keep them to myself."

"But you do have principles?"

Raven let his breath go. "Those, yes. There are things that don't change, aren't there—things like justice and honour, pride in your country and people?"

Ilona was lighting candles in the sitting-room, fat beeswax candles that she bought in a shop near the cathedral. They flared one by one as she touched a taper to them, adding an air of mystery to the darkened room. Szechenyi heaved himself to his feet and poured methylated spirit over the bed of charcoal in the brazier. The flames reddened his sallow face.

"How long will Kirstie be in London?"

Raven shrugged. "Three or four days. It depends on how long the job takes."

Szechenyi drew a rake across the charcoal, showering the patio with sparks. He moved back hurriedly to the recliner, brushing his clothes.

"I'm glad you two found one another. We've known her a long time. We think of her as one of the family."

"Don't tell her I said so," grinned Raven. "But I'm glad too."

Szechenyi hesitated. "I'd like to think of you both as friends." He looked out to sea. The sun had vanished beyond the horizon.

It was the sort of conversation that Raven found embarrassing.

"I'd better go in and change," he said awkwardly.

The two women emerged, carrying the table between them.

Kirstie had put on a pair of black trousers and a white silk shirt. Her blonde hair was pinned on top of her head. She walked past Raven, leaving him to follow Ilona into the house. It was a weird game she was playing, he decided, steering him at her friend, then complaining about the result.

The large kitchen had a bottled-gas stove, an enormous ancient refrigerator and a Fish of the World poster hanging on the whitewashed wall. It was probably colder than a frog's tit in winter, but it was a cheerful place at the moment. Ilona was at the well-scrubbed table, gutting sardines and stuffing a sprig of mint in each carcass. A cigarette was burning in an ashtray beside her. She picked it up with rubber-gloved fingers.

"What was my father talking about?"

"Nothing in particular," he answered. He opened the refrigerator and pulled the tab on a can of beer. He still had a thirst. He found himself noticing things about her that he had missed before. For instance, this trick of widening her eyes before she asked a question.

"I thought he wanted to talk to you," she said.

He sank the beer and dropped the can in the garbage pail. "Just stuff," he said, finding the wall with his shoulders. "Have you realized that Kirstie is jealous?"

She started slicing bread with firm strokes of the knife. "She's not really serious. Kirstie's far too sure of you. It's something that women do. She's going to be away for a while. She wants to put a fence around you."

"Well, I'm not too sure that I like it. It's a new experience. Did she say anything to you?"

She peeled off the rubber gloves and hung them over the taps on the sink. "Yes."

"Just 'yes'?" he said. "You're not going to tell me what?"

She piled the bread in a wicker basket. "If you want to know the truth, it's me she's worried about, not you. I already told you, she's dead sure of her husband."

"That's ridiculous," he said, shaking his head. "Why you?"

Her eyes were steady. "I think you already know the answer to that, John."

He glanced away through the window. Kirstie and Szechenyi were deep in conversation. Ilona started folding paper napkins. She broke off suddenly, looking at him again.

"Nothing in the world lasts for ever, especially love. I learned that the hard way, not that it matters. People still take the chance. I think that's what Kirstie is thinking about."

He came off the wall. "You're both being very stupid is all I can say." He picked up a radish from the bowl on the table.

"Tell me something," she asked in her deep, warm voice. "Are you my friend?"

He spoke with the burn of the radish in his mouth. "Of course I'm your friend."

"Then do something for me," she said. "My father's in serious trouble. I want you to help him."

Her face told him that she was close to tears. "I'll do whatever I can," he said. "That goes without saying."

She moved round the table and stood looking up at him. "We need your help, John."

He lifted his shoulders, aware that Kirstie was watching through the window.

"I can't do much if I don't know the problem. What is it— money?"

Her face was under control again. "I only know part of it. Papa will tell you himself. Are you hungry?"

It was a relief to talk about something as uncomplicated. "I've been hungry ever since I got here, added to which I had a leaf of lettuce for lunch."

"Go and have your bath," she suggested. "We'll eat in half an hour."

There were four bedrooms in the villa. Three of them overlooked the patio. Ilona's bedroom was on the other side of the house. The bathroom was at the end of the corridor. There were no carpets on the tiled floors, just rugs and sisal matting. The furniture was modern Portuguese, made of cheap varnished pine decorated with painted flowers. Raven showered and padded along to his bedroom. He put on his jeans and a cotton shirt and dabbed a little Paco Rabanne on his face. His mind was still with Ilona Szechenyi. She left the rented villa five days a week at eight o'clock in the morning, driving into the city and back each evening. She appeared to have no friends and was alone for twelve hours a day except for the monthly visits of her father and brother. They drank while she struggled with the accounts of the family stamp-dealing business. It seemed like one hell of an existence. There seemed to be no man in her life, though according to Kirstie there had been some Frenchman, a middle-aged rogue with panache who had borrowed money and moved along. It was a trite enough story but one that had put her in the hands of psychiatrists for the next few years. In any case, it was a waste of a desirable woman, one who deserved better.

He joined the others out on the patio. Rosemary leaves were roasting on top of the spluttering fish, the pungent smell filling the air. Ilona had tied her hair with a velvet ribbon, and her lipsticked mouth was lustrous in the candlelight. They took their places at table, Szechenyi at the head in the place of honour, Kirstie and Karolyi on his left, Ilona and Raven on the other side. Karolyi poured wine. There was a strange sense of inertia. All five seemed to be waiting for one another to do or say something.

Raven lifted his glass. "To love, honour and friendship."

There was a sudden silence, then Kirstie got hold of it. "You're making a fool of yourself," she said quietly.

Szechenyi appeared not to have heard her. He raised his own glass, the candlelight on his face. The others followed suit.

"Food!" Ilona said briskly.

She showed them all how to eat the smoking fish, holding the carcasses by the head and tail and nibbling along the backbone. They wiped their plates with the soft grey bread. It was a strange meal, with Szechenyi's morose withdrawal dampening the forced gaiety of the others. A

long hour passed before Ilona finally brought out the coffee
and brandy. Raven was grateful when Kirstie came to her
feet, stacking the empty plates and warning the others to
stay where they were.

"Nobody moves," she announced. "I do the dishes."

Raven helped her carry the table inside, leaving the
Szechenyis sitting in the glow from the dying charcoal. He
was already in bed when Kirstie came into the room. She
hung her shirt and trousers on the back of the chair and
stood at the hand-basin, brushing her teeth in her pants and
bra.

"Some meal," he said, keeping his voice down. "Like the
Last Supper."

She slammed the shutters and turned on him furiously.
"You're as much to blame as anyone. 'To love, honour and
friendship'! What was all that about?"

He folded his arms behind his head. "I don't know," he
said mildly. "It seemed a good thing at the time. A good
thing to say, I mean."

She flounced down on the side of the bed, working cream
into her face. "Why do you have to play the clown?
Couldn't you see what was going on?"

"No, I could not see what was going on," he objected.
"That's the trouble in this place. It seemed to me that I was
the only person at table behaving normally."

She aimed the soiled ball of cotton at the waste-basket.
"Stephen's in trouble."

He shifted his legs in the bed. "That much I realized, and
I'm small-minded enough to remind you that this is what I
said earlier. Ilona mentions it, you mention it, but nobody
says what the trouble is. What am I supposed to do, sit
around guessing?"

"I don't know," she replied, pulling her night-dress over
her head. "He'll tell you. He certainly won't tell me."

"Fair enough," said Raven. "When he does, maybe we
can do something about it."

She turned her long stare on him. "Why are you acting

this way, John? Is it the boat that's still bugging you? Is that why you're restless?"

He made a sound of exasperation. "In the first place, I'm not restless. And in the second place, it wouldn't be the boat if I were."

The *Western Wind* had carried his dream as far as Corfu. The cable awaiting them there had come from the biggest advertising agency in Paris, with an offer that would break new ground for Kirstie. They had talked it over, sitting outside a café on the quayside, the empty ouzo glasses collecting. The final decision had been hers. They had flown back to Paris, leaving the boat in the hands of a yacht-broker.

"You're a liar," she said. "It *is* the boat, isn't it?"

She seemed to have an obstinate wish to blame herself for the destruction of his dream. He told her the truth one more time.

"I must have said this at least on a dozen occasions. Everything I want I have. I lack nothing. Nothing at all except peace at the end of the day."

She cut the lights and crawled into bed beside him. They could hear the others talking out on the patio, but their voices were too low to be understood.

She used the tone she employed to make him feel guilty. "Come to think of it, you and Ilona are two of a kind."

"God forbid!" he said fervently. He rolled sideways, taking her face in his hands. "I hope I never wake to find another head on your pillow."

For a moment he thought that she would pull away, but her voice was soft. "You've developed a very sexy line in compliments. Good night." She turned her body so that they fitted like spoons.

Then he kissed the back of her neck where the hair was softest. "Good night."

They breakfasted out on the patio, having swum before seven o'clock. Kirstie was wearing a leaf-patterned dress and new sling-back Guccis. Her golden sun-tan made a perfect foil for the jade heart that hung between her breasts. The flight bag was all she was taking. There was everything she needed on the houseboat in London.

He finished his orange juice and wiped his mouth. "Did anyone ever tell you that you're the best-looking woman in the whole wide world?" he asked suddenly.

She put her coffee-cup down very carefully, avoiding slopping its contents.

"Only you. You usually say it when you're drunk or if you have a guilty conscience."

He could see the other three sitting at the kitchen-table. A night's rest had done nothing for Szechenyi's peace of mind. He was staring morosely in front of him.

Kirstie found her make-up. "I'm glad you're not coming to the airport," she said. "Both of us hate it in any case. All that last-minute waving and nobody knowing what to say. You'd be stuck for the rest of the day in Lisbon with nothing to do."

"That's right," he said. The sun was pleasantly warm on his back. He was still in his swim-trunks. "What would be a good time to call you?"

The green eye-shadow she was applying heightened the splash of freckles bridging her nose.

"I've got a session with the agency," she said. "A working lunch. With any sort of luck we'll start shooting this afternoon, and if we do get started I'll stay with it until the light goes. How can I give you a time? You'll just have to keep trying."

He scratched his ear, looking at her fondly. "I'm going to miss you, pussy-cat."

She turned her wrist, checking her watch. "On the off chance that you mean what you're saying, it'll take you two minutes to go to the john, another two to put on some clothes. You can still come to London if you want."

"You'd never forgive me," he smiled. "Added to which I wouldn't get a seat."

She cocked her head. "Really? And since when couldn't you get a seat on a plane? All those yarns that you spin and the name-dropping!"

"It's too much hassle," he said. "I'll just save you up in my mind."

"Like hell you will," she said, looking at the hem of her dress. "You'll have plenty to distract you."

"You disappoint me," he said sorrowfully. "I thought we'd settled all that last night."

"I was thinking of Stephen," she said. "I want you to promise me something. I want you to promise that you will help him, John. If it's money, I'll put in my share and there's no need for him to know."

"I've already told you," he answered. "I don't go back on my word. I'll do what I can, whatever it is. I can't say more."

She collected her things. The others were coming out of the house. Karolyi's plane left an hour before Kirstie's. Raven glanced across at the group.

"Someone ought to put the old man's suit in the washtub. I've counted five fresh stains since he's been here."

They started walking towards the car. "Don't forget what I told you," said Kirstie. "Ilona's special."

She wedged herself into the back of the Volkswagen, Karolyi beside her. They both carried their bags on their knees. Szechenyi was in the passenger seat next to his daughter. Kirstie snatched a kiss from her mouth with her fingers and planted it on Raven's lips.

"Call me tonight and behave yourself!"

He waited until the car was out of sight, then went into the kitchen and packed his lunch. It consisted of an apple, a banana and a hunk of the Cheddar cheese they had brought from London. He added a can of beer and a book and carried the basket down to the beach.

CHAPTER 3

Gotsek pulled the rented Fiat under a tree and stopped the motor. The quiet street ran parallel to the highway that bordered the river. Only one side was built upon. Facing the row of houses were six municipal tennis courts. Gotsek lit a cigarette, his eyes on a door thirty yards away. A limp Hungarian flag hung from a pole.

A young man emerged as Gotsek watched. He was in his early twenties, wearing a black leather bomber jacket and Easy Rider boots. A multicoloured band round his head confined his shoulder-length hair. He went past the Fiat without glancing sideways.

Water sprinklers toiled on the tennis courts. It was six o'clock and no one was playing. Gotsek crossed the street. A metal plaque screwed on the door bore the legend Hungarian Trade Delegation. Gotsek turned the handle. A fat man came into the hallway, ducking his head in greeting.

"Counselor Gotsek? Georg Nylasi!"

The Budapest accent was strong. Nylasi was built on the order of a sumo wrestler, with pale eyes set in a cheeselike face. The corduroy jacket hanging from his shoulders only partially concealed his gross, pear-shaped body.

Gotsek was familiar with the breed and disliked them intensely. Seemingly cloned in the steel towns on the Yugoslav border, they were recruited young into the KS and trained in all aspects of physical violence. Once their instruction had been completed, they killed without compunction.

Nylasi locked the street door and led the way into an

office. Shelves were laden with boxes of samples. Ball-bearings packaged in clear plastic, shirts wrapped in Cellophane, and a collection of painted wooden toys. The only decoration was a poster of the Bakony Forest.

Gotsek made no attempt to conceal his distaste for his surroundings. The trade delegation was a cynically transparent cover for Nylasi's real function as Director KS Iberian Section. The station had been transferred from Madrid to Lisbon after the revolution.

Gotsek wiped the seat of the chair with his handkerchief, aware of the other man's sardonic assessment. Gotsek was used to implied criticism. Travel had given him a taste for the trappings of capitalism, his position at the ministry the means to acquire them. It was a combination that did nothing to enhance his popularity.

He folded his panama hat and placed it on the desk. "Are we alone?"

"As good as," Nylasi answered. "We can talk in safety."

There was no sign of anyone else, but Gotsek was familiar with the way these places were run. Any member of the staff would have a double function.

Gotsek extended a hand. "I believe that you have something for me?"

Nylasi reached for a drawer, grunting with the effort. The folder he produced contained a typewritten page with a couple of photographs clipped to it. Gotsek read the information it contained.

TOP SECRET AND CONFIDENTIAL

SZECHENYI Ilona-Maria. Born Madrid 4/1/1954. Subject is of Spanish nationality, holding a passport issued in Madrid 6/22/65. Subject was educated at Saint Michael's Convent School, Cádiz, and the International School, Chateau d'Oex, Switzerland. Subject completed her education in 1969 and returned to Spain, where she lived with her parents (Q.V.) at Palo Alto, Florida,

Madrid. In 1971 subject removed to England, where she worked for an import-export firm trading with Eastern Europe. In 1973 subject opened a translation bureau in Lisbon together with Luisa Pinto, a Portuguese national. Subject entered the Clínica Galvez in July 1976, a private sanatorium specializing in the treatment of psychiatric disorders. She was discharged in October 1976. No medical record is available. Subject is a single woman with no known political affiliations. Normal banking inquiries have resulted in a negative credit rating. Subject is the owner of a blue Volkswagen convertible registered in Lisbon, January 1977 (936-MNB-2589). Subject's business address: Lusitanian Translation Services, Rossio 83 7-frente. Telephone 119-134. Home address: Vila Verde, Estrada da Sacotes, Sintra. Telephone 555-933.

One of the photographs attached was passport size. The other, a candid-camera shot, showed Ilona Szechenyi leaving the forecourt of a filling-station.

Gotsek pocketed the paper and photographs. "Is there any chance that she'd know she's been watched?"

Nylasi treated the suggestion with scorn. "You must have seen the young man, the one with the long hair?"

There was no ashtray visible. Gotsek used the empty inkwell. "Yes."

Nylasi leaned forward confidentially. "A local find. A Portuguese father, the mother's Hungarian. I'm thinking of sending him to training-school. Don't be misled by his appearance."

Gotsek's eyes followed the stream of tobacco smoke. "I asked you to find out how many people are staying in the villa."

Nylasi struggled back into an upright position. "There are five. The three Szechenyis and a couple of foreigners, a man and a woman."

"And who are these people?" Gotsek asked.

Nylasi's shrug incorporated movement of his vast belly. No matter what he did or said, his eyes retained the same awareness.

"Apparently they're friends of the girl's. British or American, Ottilio thinks. The pattern of their behaviour hasn't changed since Ottilio started his surveillance."

"Exactly what does that mean?"

"The Szechenyi girl drives into work every morning. The other two spend the day on the beach."

Gotsek's fingers sought an eyebrow, massaging it thoughtfully. Unknown factors disturbed him.

Nylasi continued. "I'm sure that you're aware that this affair has been hanging around for years. We did a project on it as long ago as nineteen seventy."

"I read the report," Gotsek said brusquely. Since his assignment, he had studied everything in the Szechenyi file. "One doesn't need a hammer to break an egg."

Nylasi's complacency faded. "The report was well received at the time. We all know the reasons why it was shelved."

It was difficult for Gotsek to hide his dislike for the other man. The KS agents he had met were unpleasantly predictable, ruthless when wielding the whip, sycophantic when deprived of it.

"Szechenyi's intelligent," said Gotsek. "He'll listen to reason. It's all that's required."

Nylasi was almost neckless. His nod brought his chin close to his breastbone.

"Ottilio will be out there again tomorrow if that's what you want."

"I want an account of these people's movements," Gotsek replied. "I drafted your instructions myself, so I know what's in them. Were they clear to you?"

"Most of them were." Nylasi's gaze was fixed like a

snake's. "There was one phrase I'm not sure about." He slid a piece of paper across the desk.

The decoded message originated in the KS headquarters in Budapest.

PROTECT AND ASSIST ADVICE

ANNOUNCE IMMINENT ARRIVAL NICHOLAS GOTSEK STOP COUNSELOR GOTSEK ACTING AS PLENIPOTENTIARY FOREIGN MINISTRY AND WILL REPORT DIRECTLY TO HIS SUPERIORS STOP NO INDEPENDENT ACTION REQUIRED EXCEPT IN CASE OF FORCE MAJEURE STOP

CADRECOMMAND

Gotsek returned the document. "What seems to be the problem?"

"*Force majeure*," said Nylasi. "I know what it says, but what does it mean?"

Gotsek took the cigarette from his mouth. "It means that in the unlikely event of my death, you'd be free to give rein to the alternative plan. Do you read much Kafka, Director?"

Nylasi locked a drawer on the slip of paper. "Kafka? No, why?"

"The art of instilling fear," Gotsek said equably. "Kafka is a past master at it."

Nylasi scribbled the name on a pad. "I shall need to know where you are staying."

"The Peninsular Hotel," answered Gotsek. The five-star rating was calculated to offend the other man's sense of propriety. "Room four-twelve. There must be no visitors and no telephone calls except in an emergency. In that case, you will make the call yourself and talk in Hungarian. If I'm out, leave a message and I will get back to you. You're sure about Ottilio?"

"Completely reliable," Nylasi said with assurance. "He's Portuguese and he knows the area. There's no problem there. How will he make his reports?"

"The same way he's been doing," said Gotsek. "I assume that you're here most of the time?"

Nylasi made the best of his answer. "You could say *all* the time. If I should happen to be absent, there'll be someone you can talk to freely. I take it that you have your means of communicating with Budapest?"

"I have," Gotsek answered.

The fat man gave it some thought. "Do you mind if I ask you a question?"

"Why not?" said Gotsek, curious about what would come next.

"It's the money," Nylasi said confidentially. "Is it true that the sum involved is really as much as they say?"

Gotsek was enjoying himself. "Somewhat less, Director, somewhat less. The legal profession is a lucrative one in Switzerland." He rose to his feet.

Nylasi struggled to follow suit. The second attempt brought him up, red-faced and breathing hard.

"Shall we meet again before you leave?"

Gotsek smiled. "I doubt it. Matters should be resolved within the next couple of days. You have been very helpful. Goodbye."

He stepped out into sunshine and the street door closed behind him.

The Avenida da Liberdade was crowded with tourists. Teenagers sprawled outside the travel agency next to the hotel, blocking the sidewalk. The Peninsular was an old-fashioned establishment popular with businessmen. The lobby was full of cigar smoke. Little appeared to have changed in half a century. Tarnished gilt ropes imprisoned thick velvet curtains. A circular leather bench, gleaming like a Cordoban saddle, surrounded the central pillar. The bell-boys wore white cotton gloves.

Gotsek rested a hand on the reception-desk. Pale eyes over a starched collar looked at him questioningly.

"Room four-twelve," Gotsek said. "Are there any messages?"

The clerk glanced at the row of pigeon-holes. "Nothing at all, Mr. Gotsek."

Gotsek collected his key from the head porter, who struck his hands together sharply. A bellboy leaped forward. Gotsek followed the youth to the elevators. Once upstairs, he bolted the door and stretched out on the bed.

Son of an itinerant Austrian carpenter and a Budapest waitress, he had been orphaned at the age of ten. At fourteen he enrolled in the Central Workers High School. Four years later he gained a place in university. He graduated at twenty-one speaking five languages fluently and entered the Foreign Ministry as a second-grade clerk. A strongly developed sense of self-preservation enabled him to avoid the traps set by Old Guard functionaries. At thirty-five he was Head of Section, with a two-room apartment in a shabby building overlooking the Danube. He skied for two weeks in February and attempted to play a 1910 Blüthner upright. Classified high in the ratings given to people having access to secret information, he was promoted to confidential aide to the minister. The appointment had taken him from East to West, counting among his missions the retrieval of a state physicist's corpse from a Viennese brothel. His entrustment with the Szechenyi project was the high-water mark of the trust and confidence placed in him.

He opened his eyes, fiddling the control of the radio until he found the sort of music he needed.

The conversation he had had with Szechenyi, presenting the alternative to co-operation, had been no idle threat. The only problem that Gotsek could see was Szechenyi's lack of stability. Drink and despair were dangerous companions.

Gotsek donned a clean shirt and made a neat knot in his black silk tie. It was still early by Portuguese standards, the restaurant half-empty.

He dined abstemiously as always, ordering a sole and sorbet with a half-bottle of the local *rosé*. He was in bed and asleep by ten o'clock.

He was shaving when the telephone rang. It was the girl on the hotel switchboard.

"Good morning, sir. I have a Mr. Molinar on the line."

"Put him on," said Gotsek, shaking the blob of shaving-cream into the basin.

It was Nylasi, his voice apprehensive. "There's something I thought you should know. I've just this minute talked to Ottilio. He's at the airport. Karolyi Szechenyi left on the plane for Madrid. The foreign woman's waiting for the flight to London."

Gotsek dried his face, still talking. "Where is Szechenyi?"

"He was with them. He's in the city somewhere with his daughter. What do you want Ottilio to do?"

"Send him home," Gotsek said promptly. An idea was forming in his mind. "I'll tell you if I need him again."

He put the phone down, thinking. That left one person still in the villa. He consulted the paper in his jacket pocket and picked up the phone. The girl on the switchboard connected him with the number he gave her.

A woman's voice answered. Gotsek spoke in English.

"I'd like to speak to Miss Szechenyi if that's possible."

"Speaking." The voice had a pleasant huskiness.

"My name is Philip Sangstrom," said Gotsek. "The Chamber of Commerce gave me your number. I have some documents that need to be translated."

"From what to what? I mean what languages?"

"English into Portuguese." A typewriter was rattling in the background.

"That's fine. How many words would that be, Mr. Sangstrom? A rough estimate."

He invented a figure. "About ten thousand, I think. I can't be sure. I don't have the documents here. They're due on the afternoon plane from New York, business papers, nothing involved."

"Well, if you can bring them in before six," she replied, "my associate can work on them tonight. We would have to charge extra, but it would mean that you'd have the papers first thing in the morning. Do you know our address?"

"I have it in front of me," he said. "Suppose we leave it like this. If you don't see me before six o'clock, you'll know that something has gone wrong. I'll let you know in any case. Is that all right?"

"Fine," she replied. Her tone held a hint of curiosity. "You pronounce my name like a Hungarian. Most foreigners seem to have difficulty."

"I have an ear," he said modestly. "But thanks, anyway." He cradled the phone and slipped on his jacket.

The Fiat was down in the basement garage, newly washed and polished. A map in the glove compartment pointed him west along the *autoroute* that went to Cascais. The car handled well and he drove without haste, turning north eight miles out of Lisbon. Another twenty minutes took him into Sintra. The road dropped sharply, offering a distant view of the Atlantic. The way ahead meandered past empty hamlets. Hens scratched in front of the white-washed cottages. Men, women and children were at work in the vineyards behind, the hobbled mules browsing.

A dirt track on the left vanished into a plantation of pine-trees. A painted sign read Vila Verde Propriedade Privada. He parked the Fiat in the shade and opened the door. His ear detected a booming sound coming at regular intervals. He started to walk down the track. The booming grew louder as he progressed. He turned the last bend and the house was in front of him.

A flight of shallow steps led to the patio. Beyond the patio wall, dunes sloped down to the beach, enclosed by two rocky headlands. The booming sound was coming from a labyrinth of caves. A naked man was lying face down on the sand, his head covered with a handkerchief.

Gotsek stepped onto the patio. The room beyond the French windows was furnished in cheap varnished pine. On the right was a kitchen with sunshine streaming through the windows. Gotsek turned his head warily. The man on the beach was still in the same position.

Gotsek called from the steps, his voice just loud enough to be heard inside the house.

"Is anyone there?" He called again without answer. He walked forward into the room, carrying his panama hat in his hand. It was the first time in his life that he had entered a house uninvited. As an occasional reader of suspense fiction, he knew the conventions.

The first bedroom he looked at was clearly Ilona Szechenyi's. A cheval-mirror reflected Gotsek in the doorway. A folded night-dress lay on the bed. There was a picture of a younger Szechenyi on the dressing-table.

Gotsek crossed the corridor. The double bed there had been neatly made. He opened the clothes-closet. A jacket and slacks hung on the rail. Gotsek read the tailor's label stitched inside the pocket.

John Raven Esquire   May 29, 1974

There was more clothing in the closet, including a woman's attire. Gotsek opened a drawer, his eye on the window. The man on the beach was still there, lying in the same position. Inside the drawer were money, keys, a plastic wallet containing credit cards, and a red leather satchel. Gotsek unzipped it. Inside was a British Airways London–Lisbon–London flight ticket, the return portion unused and undated. The passport identified the holder as John Raven, born in Sudbury, Suffolk, on August 11, 1943. The appended details gave his height as six feet three inches, no distinguishing marks and no occupation. The photograph on the adjoining page showed a man with longish grey hair

and arrogant eyes. Folded inside the passport was a piece
clipped from the society page of the Toronto *Globe and
Mail* and dated the previous year.

TORONTONIAN WEDS SCOTLAND YARD ACE

The marriage took place yesterday between Miss Kirstie Macfarlane late of Russell Hill Drive and Mr. John
Raven of London, England. Mrs. Raven was well
known here as a freelance photographer both in the
city and in Ottawa where she studied under Gerald
Karsh. For the last eleven years, she has been living
and working in Paris. Mr. Raven joined the Metropolitan Police Force at the age of twenty-one, passing
out with honors at the police college in Hartley Wint-
ney, Hampshire. Detective-Inspector Raven, as he later
became, had a brilliant career with the Serious Crimes
and Drugs squads. The recipient of various awards for
distinguished service, Mr. Raven retired prematurely in
1977. He makes his home on a converted barge moored
in London's Chelsea Reach, where the bride and groom
will reside. The honeymoon will be spent on Vancouver
Island.

The photograph inserted showed Raven and an attractive
blonde staring into the camera lens.

Gotsek put the things back as he had found them and
stepped into the corridor. There were two more doors on
the same side. The first room was empty. He opened the
second. There was a canvas bag on one of the two beds. He
tried the catch. It was locked. A quick glance through the
window reassured him and he opened the louvered clothes-
closet. There was nothing there except for a plastic shopping bag. He looked inside. At the bottom of the bag was a
.32-calibre five-shot revolver. A box of spare shells lay beside it. He pushed the closet door shut and surveyed the
rest of the room. There was no sign of Szechenyi's personal
belongings.

Gotsek was starting to sweat, unnerved by the sight of the gun. He tiptoed back along the corridor and was outside on the patio when Raven clambered over the wall. The Englishman was dressed in swim-trunks and was carrying a basket. He brushed the sand from his legs and feet, a look of surprise spreading over his face as he saw Gotsek.

Gotsek walked towards him smiling pleasantly. "Good afternoon! I was looking for Mr. Szechenyi."

Raven walked round the swing, frowning. "I'm afraid he's not here. He's in the city somewhere. He drove in with his daughter this morning. Was he expecting you?"

"No," said Gotsek, maintaining his smile. "I happened to be in Lisbon and I came by on the chance."

"Too bad!" Raven's eyes sought the steps leading into the house. "I'm afraid they won't be back until about seven. Can I offer you something to drink? Would you like to leave a note?"

"That won't be necessary," Gotsek answered. His pulse rate was beginning to slow. "Perhaps you'll be good enough to tell him I called. The name is Gotsek, Nicholas Gotsek."

"Of course!" Raven flashed a quick smile. "My name's Raven. I'm staying with his daughter. That is, my wife and I are staying. She's gone to London for a couple of days."

Gotsek lifted his hat. "I am sorry to have missed an old friend. Please say that I'll call him."

"Sure," said Raven. He glanced across at the empty carport. "Don't tell me you walked!"

Gotsek shook his head, his nerves completely under control again. "I didn't know how far it was to the house. I left my car near the road. I am sorry to have troubled you. Goodbye, Mr. Raven."

He turned to wave from the edge of the umbrella pines, but Raven was already inside the house. Gotsek sat in the car for a while taking stock. No real damage had been done and he knew who Raven was. It had to be coincidence that the man had been in the police. The reflection dissipated the last doubt in Gotsek's mind. He switched on the motor and drove back to Lisbon with the radio playing Mozart.

CHAPTER 4

It was twenty to seven when Raven looked at his watch. It was a great way to live, he decided. The minimum of conventions and nobody telling him what to do. It was the kind of freedom that well might pall, but for the moment, he was enjoying it. It was cool in the house after the heat of the beach. The telephone rang as he was putting on his jeans. He took the call in Ilona's bedroom. The night-dress smelled of the scent she used.

It was Kirstie on the line, her voice edged with impatience. "I've been trying to reach you all afternoon. Where were you?"

"On the beach," he said patiently. "How did the meeting go?"

"It went the way you might have expected," she said. "Everyone talking and no one listening. We've only just this minute finished. I'm still at the agency. A whole day wasted. I wonder why the hell I bother to do it."

"I can give you the answer on that one," he said. She sounded a little depressed. "You do it for the loot and the glory. Two thousand five hundred pounds and a double spread of Maggie Sanchez in *Vogue*. Did you look at my plants?"

"I didn't have time to go to the boat," she answered. "But I talked to Mrs. Burrows. There've been no major disasters." There was no love lost between Kirstie and the cockney charwoman who had been with Raven for years.

"I've been lying in the sun with nobody bugging me," he announced, smiling to himself. "A life of absolute peace."

Her voice was oversweet. "It's a pity I have to break it up."

"What's that supposed to mean?" he demanded.

"I'll be back on Monday," she replied.

"*Monday?*" He could hear the Volkswagen stuttering through the trees outside. "How did you manage that?"

She tinkled a laugh. "You don't sound too pleased, poor darling! Believe it or not, Maggie's agreed to work on Sunday."

"So she should, the kind of money she earns," he said.

"Simon's fixed the locations," she said. "Maggie can't do Friday, so we're shooting on Saturday and Sunday. Monday you'll have me back in your bed. Don't you find that exciting?"

"All I've been waiting for," he retorted. Ilona Szechenyi was standing in the doorway. "There's someone here who wants to talk to you," he said to Kirstie and held out the phone to Ilona. "It's Kirstie."

He rose from the bed, having no wish to be there while they traded their girlish secrets. "Where's your father?"

Ilona swung her hair back with a self-conscious gesture. "Out on the patio."

Szechenyi was on the swing, looking out across the placid waste of sunlit water.

Raven waved cheerfully. "Hi! You had a visitor this afternoon. Someone called Gotsek. He was sorry to have missed you. He said that he'll be in touch."

Szechenyi was on his feet in a flash, stammering as he tried to speak. "Did he go in the house?" he finally managed.

"I've no idea," answered Raven. "He was standing here when I came up from the beach. Is something the matter?"

Szechenyi brushed by, moving hurriedly. Raven followed him into the villa. Szechenyi relocked his canvas bag and went to the clothes-closet.

"What the hell are you doing with that thing?" said

Raven, staring at the revolver Szechenyi was holding. Ilona had come into the room. Her father sank down on the bed. She took the gun from his hand and returned the plastic bag to the clothes-closet.

"Gotsek's been here," he said, looking up at her. His Adam's apple bulged in his scrawny neck. He looked at that moment an old and defeated man.

"I think you had better go," he said shakily, speaking to Raven. "Just pack your things and go. Ilona will drive you into the city."

"Go?" Raven repeated, looking from father to daughter. "I just don't believe what I'm hearing. What's happened, what's going on?"

She crossed the room to her father's side, tight-lipped and silent. Her hand found his shoulder and his chin lifted.

"It is a long and dangerous story. Ilona only knows part of it. We have no right to involve you."

Raven was beginning to run out of patience.

"I appreciate your concern, but isn't it a bit late for that?"

Ilona spoke in Hungarian. Whatever she said had the effect of pulling Szechenyi into a semblance of dignity.

"You are right," he said. "You are a friend and I owe you an apology."

"You can skip the apologies," Raven answered. "I thought I'd already made myself clear. If you're in trouble, I may be in a position to help." The only thing he could think of was money, that Gotsek was some kind of debt-collector.

Ilona touched her father's ashen cheeks with her finger-tips. "I think it's better if we go outside. This place is giving me the creeps."

Szechenyi struggled up. The last few minutes had aged him. He brought the canvas bag with him. It was low tide, and the beach glistened with iridescent blobs of jellyfish. Ilona came from the kitchen carrying a beer for Raven, brandy and water for her father. She sat on the swing beside Raven, watching her father unfasten his travelling-bag. Szechenyi produced a bundle of papers.

"Do you read French?" he said to Raven.

Raven nodded. The Hungarian selected a couple of documents from his bundle and passed them to Ilona. She read without comment and gave them to Raven.

The first was a letter written a month ago.

Banque Suisse et Ottomane
Place des Vosges
Geneva

M. le Comte Szechenyi
Aux soins du Maitre Pasquale Palau
Córdoba 18
Madrid
Espagne

M. le Comte:

I am instructed by my board of directors to inform you that a decision in your favour was reached by the Federal Court in Berne on June 12, 1983. We are advised by our legal staff that this decision is irrevocable under Swiss law.

Due to the delicate nature of the final settlement of your account with us, I am instructed to deal with the matter in person. To this end, I propose to travel to Madrid, arriving on June 23. I shall be staying at the Palace Hotel and will be grateful if you can attend there at 4 P.M. on June 24, bringing with you evidence of certain confidential matters and the documents produced at the time of opening your account with us.

Should these arrangements fail to meet with your approval, kindly advise me by telephone. The bank, of course, holds itself in readiness to wait upon you at any alternative time and place of your choosing.

Deign to accept our most distinguished sentiments. I remain your devoted servant.

Pierre de Fonjallez
Vice-President

Raven exchanged the letter for the newspaper clipping.

GOLD FROM THE SKY

Berne, June 16

A decision was reached in the Federal Court today finally resolving the ownership of approximately U.S. $17 million. The money is the product of a shipment of gold bullion flown into Switzerland in 1945, shortly before the collapse of the Horthy régime. The bullion was deposited in the Geneva branch of the Banque Suisse et Ottomane by the then Hungarian air attaché in Madrid, Colonel Count Szechenyi. Five weeks later the new Hungarian Government contested legal title to the account in the cantonal court. The claim was opposed by the Banque Suisse et Ottomane in the name of the titular holder. These proceedings were the opening salvoes in a legal battle that has been waged in our courts over a period of thirty-seven years.

Judge Halbherr, handing down the final ruling of the Federal Court yesterday, stated that the issue involved struck at the very heart of Swiss banking. A decision in favour of the plaintiffs would jeopardize accounts held by foreign institutions and residents who relied upon the probity of our financial institutions. We have a world-wide and justified reputation for the integrity of our banking system, and it is essential that this reputation should be preserved. Ownership of the account would be vested in the person of Count Szechenyi, the original depositor.

The length of this case has established legal precedent, according to banking circles here in Berne. Estimated

costs could be as high as U.S. $3.5 million. A spokes-
man for the Banque Suisse et Ottomane declined to say
whether Count Szechenyi was still living.

Raven returned the papers, seeing no more than an old
man in a wrinkled stained suit. It was difficult to hide his
disbelief.

"You mean you've lived with this on your mind for all
those years and not even a word to your family?"

Ilona moved beside him. There was a hint of bitterness in
her voice. "The first I heard of it was yesterday. My brother
still doesn't know."

Szechenyi shook his head sadly. "Nobody seems to understand. What happened in Switzerland no longer seemed real
as the years went by. Even when the man arrived from the
bank, it was still hard to believe what had happened. You
see, the money was never mine in the first place. My orders
were to fly six boxes of gold from Budapest to Switzerland.
The gold was converted to dollars and that was that. I was
no more than an instrument."

"That's as may be," said Raven. "But you're the rightful
owner, legally at any rate. You made the deposit."

Szechenyi moved his head in agreement. "It was pure
chance. Fate. Call it what you will. Only three people knew
of my mission. A representative of the Bank of Hungary was
supposed to fly on the plane with the gold. He collapsed
from a heart attack twenty minutes before take-off. There
was no time to arrange for a substitute. That left me."

Raven's mind sought the map. "Didn't you have to take
the plane back to Hungary?"

Szechenyi moved scarecrow shoulders. "The plane was
detained in Geneva. I returned to Madrid. My orders came
from the Regent himself. The Russians invaded a week
later."

"And you stayed in Spain?"

Szechenyi's hand crept towards his empty glass. "I stayed.

The communists were in control of the country by now. A week later I heard that the account had been blocked."

There was something about the story that Raven found strange. "But you must have thought about what would happen to the money. You must have had some idea what you'd do if the courts swung your way?"

Szechenyi offered a shaky smile. "Like starting a revolution? There were other things on my mind by then. My parents and my sister had been murdered. I was a man with nowhere to go. I just had to get on with living the best way I knew. All the rest became a sort of dream. I've already told you, it was still a dream when Fonjallez came to Madrid. The man you saw this afternoon turned it into reality."

Ilona's hands moved nervously. "Gotsek works for the Hungarian Government. He went to see Papa in Madrid a few days ago. They want the return of the money."

"Well, that's too bad," answered Raven. "The courts have decided against them. Did you know that Gotsek was in Portugal?"

Szechenyi's liver-spotted hand trembled as he lifted the brandy bottle. "No. That was a turn of the screw, his visit here. He wanted to make his point. They've offered me half a million dollars and the chance to spend it in safety. Otherwise . . ." He rolled his thumb down.

"That's ridiculous," Raven said promptly. "All you have to do is pick up the phone and inform the police that you're being threatened."

"No police!" There was a hint of desperation in Szechenyi's voice. "I know these people. They never give up. It may be someone like Gotsek at first, an educated man offering a compromise. If that fails, they resort to other methods of persuasion. Let me tell you about Professor Teleki. He was one of the lucky ones to get out in 1956. Somebody like Gotsek tracked him to Florida, where he was working on the space programme. They offered him a chair in Budapest

University, his own laboratories. *Carte blanche.* He refused and went to the FBI. Teleki's wife and son were killed in a car accident two weeks later. The brake cables had been cut."

Raven reached for a cigarette. He was beginning to understand. "Are you telling me seriously that your life is in danger?"

"Not mine," said Szechenyi, looking at his daughter. "But the children's lives, yes. You only see the killer once."

Raven felt Ilona's body shiver beside him. "This is nonsense," he said. "You're a man of good character and you're rich. It's a formidable combination. Why are you scared of going to the police?"

Szechenyi put his empty glass down. "Because I know what would happen."

Raven changed tack. Fear of the police was something he knew about. "OK, forget the police. There are other people we can go to, people who are trained to handle this kind of thing."

"Someone like the FBI?" Szechenyi asked sombrely. "People are being killed in broad daylight, bundled into planes and kidnapped! I never thought that it would come to this, but it has. It isn't myself I care about. The important thing is my children."

Raven glanced at Ilona. "You seem to have talked to her about things. OK, about part of it. Why not Karolyi?"

Szechenyi's explanation was that of a man who has thought long on the subject.

"You must understand, John. I wanted to speak to Ilona first. Karolyi has always been different. Even as a boy he was different. You see, he resented the way we lived, wanted the things that his friends had. He hasn't changed. You must have noticed when Kirstie and you were talking, his reaction. Those are the places he dreams about, the sort of life he would wish to have. London, Paris, night-clubs. Models. He feels he has been cheated."

"Then he's daft," said Raven. He moved away slightly. Ilona's body was almost touching his. "I don't suppose Kirstie and I have been in a night-club in eighteen months. We do our shopping in Safeways, and the models get their glamour from their make-up boxes. Anyway, the ones that Kirstie uses."

The drink from Szechenyi's glass was slopping onto his trousers. He seemed not to notice it.

"Will you help us?" he asked shakily.

"You get to know me better," said Raven, "and you'll realize that I don't make promises lightly. Not that kind of promise, anyway."

Szechenyi brushed at the vein near his temple. "Will you go to Madrid with Ilona? I want you to bring Karolyi back with you. I can't let her go alone. I need my family here, John. Whatever decision has to be made must be made by us all. I have imposed my will upon them all too often."

Raven turned his head slowly. "Is this your idea?" he said to Ilona. "Me going to Madrid with you?"

"I don't want to go alone," she reiterated. "Karolyi will listen to me. I can make him see sense."

"You can?" he said dourly. "Well, I wish to God someone would make *me* see sense. Why not just pick up the phone and call him?"

Her father came to her defence. "If you do not wish to go, I will go myself."

The words and the way they were said had a disturbing effect upon Raven. What they were asking was little enough.

"When were you thinking of leaving?"

Father and daughter exchanged quick glances. "As soon as possible," said Szechenyi. "Now! There is no time to waste."

Raven nodded, thinking. Madrid had to be a six-hour drive, probably more in the clapped-out Volkswagen.

"OK," he said to Ilona. "You'd better get your things together."

She threw her arms round him impulsively and hurried into the house.

Relief flooded into Szechenyi's worn features. "You still think that I am doing the wrong thing, don't you?"

Raven moved his shoulders. "I'm finding all this pretty hard to take in. You want me to go to Madrid with Ilona, I'll do it. But don't ask me if it's right or wrong."

Szechenyi stood up, his manner a great deal calmer than it had been. "I have to do it this way. Have no fear for me. There is no real danger while they are waiting for my decision."

Raven matched steps with the older man as they crossed the patio to the house.

"I have contacts in London," he said on impulse. "You can be there in a matter of hours, all three of you. I can make sure that you're taken care of, hidden away where no one can get at you."

Szechenyi slowed. "You are a good man, a true friend, but you do not understand. It is a different world, John. There is no room in it for that kind of thinking."

"Whatever you say," shrugged Raven. Illogical or not, the prospect of driving to Madrid with Ilona had begun to excite him.

He stuffed a razor, tooth-brush and a clean pair of socks into the red satchel and collected his passport and money. Ilona had changed into jeans. A suede jacket hung on the back of a chair.

"I'd like to call Kirstie," he said.

She was doing her face in the mirror and watched as he sat on the bed. He picked up the phone and made the connection.

"It's me," he said when he heard Kirstie's voice. "Something's come up. I can't talk about it now, but we've got to go to Madrid to fetch Karolyi. We'll be back in the morning, OK?"

"Who's 'we'?" she asked. Voices sounded in the background.

"Ilona and me. Look, I can't explain but it's important."

"I'll bet," she said starchily. "Be sure to enjoy yourselves." She put the phone down before he could answer.

"Shit!" he said, jiggling the receiver, but the line was dead.

Ilona picked up her jacket and shoulder-bag. "Problems?"

Tension showed in her eyes, the nervous movement of her mouth.

"Just don't get married," he said with feeling. "It's the quick road to disillusionment."

Szechenyi was waiting at the carport. "Take care of her," he said to Raven as his daughter settled behind the wheel. Raven moved in beside her. Szechenyi stayed with his hand raised in farewell until a bend placed him out of sight.

"Now you can see why my father drinks," she said quietly.

Raven wound down his window. "There's always a reason," he answered.

CHAPTER 5

Ilona pulled the Volkswagen to the kerb. It was half past six in the morning, with the sun rising behind the trees that lined the boulevard. They had taken turns driving through the night, pushing the small machine along mountain highways that were still edged with snow.

"Home Sweet Home!" said Ilona, pointing down the grassy slope. Four grim tower blocks connected by covered walkways rose from a concrete car-park.

It was worse than Raven had expected. Early morning workers in the nearby café were waiting for the Metro station to open.

"It's not even seven o'clock," Raven objected, looking at his watch. "We can't go crashing in at this time of the morning."

She wadded the tissue she had cleaned her face with and stuffed it into the ashtray.

"We can. At least, *I* can. You'd better wait here. Get yourself some coffee. There's bound to be an argument."

She reached for her bag on the rear seat.

"How do you mean, an argument?" he asked. "I thought you two were close."

She spoke from superior knowledge. "That's what my father likes to think. You know, the closely knit family and all the rest. The truth is, I've made a mess of my life and Karolyi has no time for failures. Especially when it's his sister."

A traffic cop roared by, the wheels of his motorcycle hugging the white dividing line. Ilona opened her door.

"He'll move fast enough when he hears what I have to say."

Raven watched her down the slope and walked into the nearby café. The men there were drinking anise. He bought himself a doughnut and a carton of chocolate and took them back to the car. Twenty minutes passed before Ilona appeared at the foot of the hill. She was a hundred yards away, alone and clearly in a state of panic, running knock-kneed and with her head down. He wrenched the door open and raced to meet her. She stumbled into his arms, her eyes wide with fear.

"I can't open the door. Something's wrong with the lock. It's jammed and Karolyi won't answer the bell."

They hurried back, Ilona leading him down a dimly lit passageway into a cheerless lobby with vast bare windows. The elevator rose and she gave him a key, pointing at the lock. He bent to take a closer look. Something was wedged in the keyhole.

"Have you got a pin?" he said over his shoulder. "Something with a point?"

She groped in her bag and came up with a nail-file. He used it to pick out the sliver of matchstick. He took the key and the door opened easily. They stepped into a small hallway. The radio was playing in the neighbouring apartment. The curtains were drawn in the next room, making it difficult to see.

Raven took a tentative step forward. "Karolyi?" There was no reply. Ilona pointed at the half-open door. He moved with caution, calling again, Ilona close on his heels. The door swung open under his touch. It was dark in the room and there was a strong smell of alcohol. A bottle rolled underfoot as Raven took another step. His eyes focused gradually. A body was lying face down on the floor between the bed and the window. Raven wrenched the curtain back. Daylight flooded in, revealing the gruesome scene. The sheets on the bed were drenched with blood, the floor spattered. Raven pushed Ilona out of the room and turned the body over. Karolyi's unbuttoned pyjama jacket was crimson. The skin over his heart cavity showed a purple-rimmed puncture. Raven felt for a pulse and found none. The flesh was limp but warm.

Raven turned the body over on its back again, his mouth suddenly dry. He went to the doorway. Ilona was sitting on the couch in the living-room.

"He's dead," said Raven. "We're going to have to call the police."

She shook her head, refusing to accept what he said, just staring at him. "We have to call the police," he repeated.

The word galvanized her into action, and she reached the phone before he did, pinning the instrument down with both hands.

"No!"

"Are you out of your mind?" he said. "Your brother's been murdered!"

She answered with quiet desperation, her eyes filled with tears. "For God's sake, John, don't! You'll destroy us completely."

The cloying smell of blood had invaded the living-room, turning his stomach. "What the hell are you trying to say to me?"

She was still clinging to the phone. "Don't you understand? Can't you see what this is? It's a warning! You're supposed to know about these things. If you call the police, you'll have two more deaths on your conscience. My father's and mine."

He looked beyond her into the kitchen, sweat gluing his shirt to his back. There was no indication that the flat had been robbed, nothing worth stealing as far as he could see. Whoever had been there had come with murder in mind. He drew a glass of water from the kitchen tap. Ilona followed, unwilling to let him out of her sight.

"I'm pleading for our lives," she urged.

He wiped his mouth on the back of his hand. The sound of a car being started came through the open window. He watched as the vehicle was driven up the slip-road to the boulevard. It was a quarter to seven by the alarm clock on the dresser.

"What do you want me to do?" he asked quietly.

She put a hand on his arm, matching his tone. "I want to get out of here quickly. If we leave by the fire-escape no one will see us."

He made the wrong choice for the right reason, compassion overriding all other emotions. He grabbed a rag from the sink and backtracked through the apartment, wiping all the surfaces that either of them might have touched. He closed the curtains in Karolyi's bedroom and motioned Ilona into the hallway.

He found himself whispering, "Take off your shoes."

She slipped them off, steadying herself against the wall. He pulled her sun-glasses out of her shoulder-bag and fitted them on her face. The pulse in her throat was beating erratically. He brought his mouth close to her ear. Someone was moving about in the neighbouring apartment.

"As soon as I nod, you run! Wait for me at the end of the corridor."

He opened a crack in the door. Light streamed along the empty corridor. He moved his head quickly. She slipped past, carrying her shoes, her hair swinging as she ran. A faint clang sounded as she moved onto the fire-escape. He closed the door gently behind him, using his sleeve as a glove. He followed her down the corridor, his sneakers squeaking on the composition flooring. She was waiting on the stone steps outside, still holding her shoes. They negotiated the way down to street level without seeing anyone. He lifted the bar on the exit door. There was no one in sight except a couple of men climbing the grassy slope towards the Metro station.

"Stay close and walk normally," Raven warned.

By the time they reached the Volkswagen, the Metro was open. He opened the near side door.

"I'll drive," he said, squeezing behind the wheel.

She slipped in beside him. The café was thronged, the neighbourhood coming to life.

"We've got to get out of here," he said. "I must be out of my mind."

"Everything's going to be all right," she said.

He glanced sideways, sweating and unsure of himself, amazed at her sudden composure. The pupils of her eyes were brilliant. People reacted in odd ways to tragedy, but her face was devoid of all feeling.

"He's dead," she said as though reading his thoughts. "There's nothing we can do about it. There's a motel I know on the way to the airport. We can clean up and call my father from there."

He turned the ignition key. They drove twelve miles along the Barajas highway, turning off onto a strip of blacktop that led under a plaster archway. White cabins glittered in the early sunlight. A couple of peacocks strutted across the lawn in front of the office. Curtains moved as the car drew up.

"I'll take care of it," she said quickly. "Give me your passport."

"To make a telephone call?" he asked incredulously.

"We'll have to check in," she said. He gave her the document, his eyes following her as she walked over the grass. There were no other cars in sight. The place looked empty. She was back in a couple of minutes, holding a door key. They walked down a concrete pathway bordered by roses. There was a small pool surrounded by thatched parasols and shabby garden furniture.

Ilona unlocked a cabin. There were two single beds inside, a telephone on the table between them. Bullfight prints hung on the walls. There was a drinks dispenser and a coin-operated television set. Raven threw his red leather satchel on the bed by the window.

"You're certainly full of surprises. I'll say that much for you."

She hung her shoulder-bag on the back of a chair and shook her hair free.

"You mean about being here? I'm a woman and I'm frightened." She gave him a long, cool look. "I can think of other reasons if I have to."

He let it go, unwilling to pursue what he thought she meant. He took his razor and tooth-brush from his satchel.

"I'm going to take a bath."

The first burst of water ran rusty, then steam gushed. He undressed and lowered himself into the tub. He could hear her on the phone, speaking in Hungarian. He shaved and wrapped himself in the bath-sheet. Ilona was sitting on her bed in front of a tray loaded with fruit, toast and coffee. She gave him a plate and cup.

"I talked to my father," she said. "It wasn't easy. I wanted to be there, holding him tight."

She was a weird combination, he thought. As capable of showing emotion as of hiding it.

"So what's going to happen?" he asked.

"He's taking the next plane to Madrid. He wants us to stay here. He'll call us from the airport. He's going straight to the apartment."

His cup clattered as he pushed it aside. "Then *he'll* have to call the police."

Her eyes were steady. "He says that it's better this way."

"And Gotsek?"

She moved her shoulders expressively. "Gotsek's name has to be kept out of it."

Raven came to his feet. "My brain's not functioning properly. I have to get some rest."

He dropped the damp bath-sheet on the floor and crawled in between sheets smelling of sun and garden. She collected the breakfast things and put the tray outside the door. Then she drew the curtains, making the room dark and cool. Seconds later, she was in bed beside him, pulling the sheet up so that only her hair and eyes were showing. He reached across to take his cigarettes from the table. She snatched them quickly and sailed them across the room.

"Just what the hell are you doing?" he demanded.

She pushed herself upright, letting the sheet fall.

"I want you to make love to me."

"*Love,*" he repeated, playing for time.

"I can think of a coarser expression," she said, locking her hands behind her head. "What's the matter, don't you fancy me? Or is it because of my brother? Or maybe it's Kirstie, my oldest and dearest friend?"

He swung himself out of the bed and retrieved his cigarettes. The flame flared in the darkened room. Her voice was suddenly sweet and submissive.

"May I have one too, please?"

He lit it for her and got back in bed. She blew a thin stream of smoke at the ceiling.

"OK, let's talk. Why do you think that I live alone? I left home because of my father's obsession with his family. Nothing else mattered for as long as I can remember. It was even worse when my mother was alive. You stick together in spite of everything, suffer if necessary. I just couldn't go on like that. Spain's full of daughters making sacrifices for the family. They finish up with no chance of ever having one of their own."

It was a long time since a woman had opened up to him in this way. Kirstie's emotional secrets were strictly for private consumption.

He shook his head, embarrassed and sorry for her, yet unable to find the right words to express his feelings.

"I want freedom," she told him. "I've tried the alternative. It's years ago now. I had an affair with someone. It ended disastrously. So much for love."

He settled his head on the pillow, still watching her eyes. "People will tell you it's an illusion, that nothing lasts forever including love."

"And they'd be right." Her deep voice was emotionless.

He reached out again, this time for the ashtray. "Just what kind of a woman are you?"

"The usual kind," she replied. "One who needs reassuring that she *is* a woman."

"You're wasting your life," he said quietly.

She thumbed her cigarette into the ashtray with sudden decision. "*This* is real," she said, running her hands over her chest.

They lay for a while in silence, then her fingers found the back of his neck. She pulled his head up slowly until their mouths met. She pushed the sheet back, impatiently taking the initiative. Her long hair veiled his face and he lost count of time. Neither life nor death mattered now.

It was half past one by his watch when he woke in damp sheets. He had sweated heavily. The curtains were still closed. Ilona was in the bathroom. Guilt and apprehension crowded into his mind and he reached for a cigarette. The bathroom door opened as he swung out of bed. Ilona emerged, naked except for a towel wrapped around her head like a turban. They passed each other like strangers who meet in a doctor's surgery. He shut the bathroom door and stood in the shower, gasping as ice-cold needles of water covered his body.

She was brushing her wet hair when he returned to the bedroom.

"No recriminations!" she warned. "And please, no soul-searching!"

"I'd intended neither," he said. "My mind was on food." It was difficult to realize that this was the woman he'd slept with. There was no suggestion of sensuality about her.

She turned, tilting her head as she looked at him. "Friends?" she asked, smiling.

He pulled on his jeans and his socks. "Friends," he agreed.

CHAPTER 6

Szechenyi climbed into the cab, an old and deeply shocked man clinging to the remnants of his life. His brain had been prepared for disaster, but his son's death was an act of gratuitous cruelty. Gotsek must have had it in mind from the beginning.

The cabdriver slowed, aiming the question at the rearview mirror. "We are in Florida, señor. Where exactly do you want me to stop?"

"Let me out here," said Szechenyi.

He walked through the park gates. It was siesta time and the grassy slope was deserted. The elevator gates opened as Szechenyi crossed the lobby. The building superintendent came towards him, an ill-favoured man in a beret and overalls.

"Just the man I wanted to see," said García. "Someone telephoned my flat half an hour ago. A man. He wanted to know how he could get in touch with you. He'd already tried your number. I said you were probably away."

Szechenyi forced the semblance of a smile. García was a confirmed busybody. It was important to act naturally.

"Did he leave a name?"

García shook his head. "No. But I can tell you this much, he was a foreigner."

Szechenyi opened the elevator gates. "You don't look well," said García. "Are you feeling all right?"

"I'm tired," said Szechenyi, closing the gates.

García stared through the grillework. "Is your son still in Portugal?"

"He came back yesterday." Szechenyi pressed the button and the cage began its ascent.

Sunshine shafted along the corridor. The floor had been mopped and was still drying. He let himself into his apartment and stood in the darkened hallway. The curtains were drawn in all the rooms. There was no sound at all. He moved forward slowly, beginning to tremble as a fetid odor invaded his nostrils. He pushed the half-open door and the room took on shape. A cloud of flies rose, buzzing as he drew back the curtains. He looked from his son's body to the blood-stained bed. The table was overturned. He covered the corpse with a blanket and walked back to the sitting-room, tears streaming down his face. He picked up the phone and dialled Emergency.

"I'm speaking from the Palo Alto Apartments in Florida. Apartment G-26. My name is Stephen Szechenyi. My son has been killed. Yes, I will wait here, of course."

He replaced the phone and walked through to the kitchen. The brandy bottles in the cupboard were empty. He drained the remnants into a glass and sat by the window, watching the slip-road. The minutes dragged. Suddenly, he heard the wail of a siren in the distance. The volume increased and a police car appeared, hurtling down the incline.

Szechenyi hauled himself up and opened the front door. The first man out of the elevator was blond and sun-tanned, wearing linen slacks and a cotton shirt. His partner was the archetypical plainclothesman, older and easily forgotten. The building superintendent tagged along behind the two men, his nose thin with excitement. Doors were opening all along the corridor. Heads peered out. García bustled forward importantly, pointing at Szechenyi.

"That's him there!"

"Captain Alatren, Criminal Investigation." The blond man's eyes moved restlessly, looking beyond Szechenyi, probing the interior of the apartment. "You are Señor Sze-chenyi?"

Szechenyi stepped aside, allowing the detectives to enter. Alatren closed the door firmly in the superintendent's face.

"Where is the body?" he said to Szechenyi.

The three men moved into the bedroom. Alatren removed the blanket. His fingers touched the dead man's wrist briefly. He rose, wiping his hand on his handkerchief. Commotion had broken out in the corridor. People were shouting to one another.

"Get rid of all that!" Alatren ordered.

His companion hurried to the front door. The noise ceased abruptly. Alatren went to the window.

"What have you touched since you found the body? Were the curtains like this?"

"I opened them," Szechenyi answered. "The only other thing that I touched was the blanket."

"Where's your phone?"

Szechenyi led the way. The police-captain let light into the sitting-room. He dialled, giving Szechenyi's address and telephone number. A machine-gun rattle of Spanish followed.

"Homicide. Get hold of the Scene-of-Crimes Squad and the medical examiner. I want them here now!" His hand shot out at Szechenyi. "Passport!"

Szechenyi groped in his jacket. Alatren examined the passport carefully, his tongue clicking surprise. He switched his gaze from the passport to its owner.

"You are *Spanish*, señor?" The question was close to incredulity.

"I am naturalized," said Szechenyi. "The details are all there."

Alatren patted the back of the sofa. "Sit down, señor. Make yourself comfortable."

Szechenyi crossed the room with the gait of a sleep-walker. Alatren sat down beside him.

"Tell me about it, señor. I understand that the dead man was your son?"

Szechenyi covered his eyes with his hand, struggling to speak. If ever he needed a drink, it was now.

"I'm sorry," was all he could manage.

"Take your time," said Alatren. He rose suddenly, ranging the room, scrutinizing objects without touching them. He lit a Ducado and flipped the spent match through the open window. He stood with his back to it. "Does anyone else live here with you?"

Szechenyi shook his head wearily. "My wife is dead. There are only three of us left. My daughter lives in Portugal. We had been visiting her. My son returned yesterday."

Alatren was speaking with the sun behind him. A small bald patch gleamed at the back of his head.

"And you?"

"I stayed. There were things that I had to discuss with my daughter. I came here straight from the airport."

"And what time was that?" Szechenyi was sitting between the two officers. Their eyes sought one another constantly as though in confirmation of some grave suspicion.

Szechenyi plucked his trousers nervously. "It was after five when we landed. The plane was late. I missed the morning flight. I managed to get a seat on the plane that goes on to Rome."

Alatren appeared to be running the scene in his head. "You left the cab where?"

"On the boulevard. It is my habit to walk down the hill. All I had was that bag." Szechenyi nodded at the canvas holdall in the hallway.

The other officer spoke for the first time. "Did you see anyone you knew on the way up?"

"The building superintendent, that's all."

"Where was he?"

"Coming out of the elevator."

Alatren guided him on. "Was your front door open or shut?"

"It was shut," said Szechenyi. "I'd no idea that anything was wrong until I let myself in. It was the smell . . ." he broke off, closing his eyes.

He opened them to find Alatren watching him narrowly. "I went into Karolyi's bedroom and found him there on the floor. I didn't want to see him like that. That's why I covered him with the blanket."

"And you're positive you touched nothing else?" asked Alatren. "Think hard! It could be important."

Szechenyi bent his head in thought. Each question, each answer, endangered him.

"The curtains, that's all," he said finally. "I couldn't have been in the bedroom more than a couple of minutes. My first thought was to call the police."

Alatren nodded at the door opposite. "Who sleeps in there?"

"I do," said Szechenyi.

Alatren's eyes were still restless. "What about valuables? Do you keep anything valuable on the premises?"

"Nothing at all. We have a small stamp-dealing business. You could leave the front door open when we first came here. It isn't like that any more. What little there is of value is kept in the safe at the office."

Alatren slanted his gaze along the surface of the table and did the same with the top of the television set.

"Now there's a thing! The table's been wiped, but there's dust on the top of the television. Who does your cleaning?"

"A neighbour. She comes in on Mondays. There isn't much to clean. Our clothes and sheets go to the laundry."

Alatren's quest took him into Szechenyi's bedroom. He was in there alone for fully five minutes before emerging. He opened the windows to their full limit.

"This place is going to be like a madhouse in a few minutes. You won't like what you see, I'm afraid. Palau?"

His subordinate came off the wall. "Captain!"

"Stay on here until the others arrive," ordered Alatren. "We'll be at Central."

He picked up Szechenyi's flight bag and motioned him into the hallway. A couple of women were still loitering outside in the corridor.

Alatren looked at them sternly. "I advise you to get back inside, ladies. The show is over. There is nothing more to see."

The two men walked to the elevator. Once out in the open, Alatren drew a deep breath.

"It never fails. One minute you're alive, the next you are dead. No fanfare, nothing. Just the curtain is drawn." His expression changed as he saw García. The building superintendent was making a show of sweeping the forecourt. Alatren beckoned him across. "You!" he barked. "Name?"

García squared his shoulders, assuming a military stance with his broom. "Enrique García, señor!"

Alatren edged a little closer. "And what are your hours of duty, Enrique García?"

García's smile was ingratiating. "They are all too long, Señor Capitán! I work hard for little pay from eight in the morning until eight at night."

"Where do you sleep?"

García nodded back in the direction of the lobby. "I have a flat in the basement, señor."

"Are you responsible for security?"

The word provoked an acid look. "There *is* no security. I cannot be everywhere. People walk in off the street. They steal light bulbs, newspapers, mail, whatever they can get their hands on. I have enough to do just minding my own business."

Alatren grabbed the superintendent by the overalls and rocked him gently.

"I know your kind of business, Enrique García. A little bit of pimping on the side, buying and selling things that are brought to you. Drugs, in all probability. Where are the passkeys kept?"

García's face had turned a shade of yellow. "On a board in my room," he stammered. "There is one for each floor in case of emergency."

Alatren removed his hand and wiped his fingers fastidiously. The driver of the police car was leaning against his vehicle, watching.

"Who was in Señor Szechenyi's apartment?" Alatren demanded.

García swallowed painfully. "No one, señor. I swear it. I mean, the passkeys have not been touched since last week. There was a flood in one of the flats. I had to deal with it."

"Do you live alone?"

"I am a bachelor," answered García. "A member of Catholic Action." He felt for the badge pinned on the bib of his overalls.

"Catholic Action?" Alatren repeated bleakly. "Then you are vigilant for signs of wrongdoing, my friend. Tell me who you saw in the building today. Strangers."

García was no match for authority and started to stammer again. "The gentleman who visits C-10, that's all. The señorita gives lessons in English."

"Can you read and write, Enrique García?"

The superintendent was still holding his broom at attention. "I did my military service, Señor Capitán. I have a certificate of proficiency in reading and writing."

"Good," said Alatren. "Then this is what you must do. I want you to make a full report of your day on paper, a detailed account of what you have done since leaving your bed this morning. Make a note of anyone you saw or spoke to and have it ready when I come back."

He walked Szechenyi across to the police car. They drove south for half an hour, the radio chattering, the three men silent. It was the first time in his life that Szechenyi had been in police custody. He assumed that he *was* in custody.

Alatren still had his passport. They drove through tall iron gates into a courtyard shaded by chestnut-trees. The weathered stone building had once been a monastery. An armed policeman in uniform standing outside a sentry-box snapped a salute at Alatren. The police-captain led the way through an inner courtyard bordered by cloisters, Szechenyi's flight bag tucked under his arm. The Hungarian's feet were beginning to drag. Typewriters clattered behind closed doors. A statue pointed the way up a wide stone staircase.

Alatren opened a door. The room had once been used as a store of some kind. A fly-spotted picture of King Juan Carlos hung on the whitewashed wall. The only furniture was a plank table and three wooden chairs. The windows were dirty and barred. Alatren lowered them as far as they would go. The air in the room was oppressive.

"I'm sorry about this," he said amiably. "Someone else in my office. We can talk here in private. It's just a formality. We'll get you out of here as soon as possible. Would you like a coffee?"

Szechenyi sneezed suddenly, goggling with amazement. "I think I'd like a brandy if that is possible."

"That is certainly possible," Alatren said. "How about something to eat?"

"Just the brandy," said Szechenyi, making fists of his fingers. He was out of his depth and drowning.

Alatren spoke from the doorway. "I won't be a minute." He disappeared, leaving the door ajar.

Below the window was a yard with a crouching fig-tree enclosed by a moss-covered wall. The complex of cloisters and corridors led to a common exit. There was no other way out.

Alatren returned with a glass of brandy. "Drink this," he said, putting the glass on the table. "It'll settle your stomach."

Szechenyi drained it at a gulp. He wiped his mouth, aware that his handkerchief was filthy.

Alatren offered his amiable smile. "I'm going to have to leave you alone for a while. There is nothing to be afraid of, Señor Szechenyi. Would you like me to call a friend, someone you'd like to know what is happening?"

Szechenyi spoke with the hollow voice of a very old man. "There is no one."

Alatren closed the door again. Szechenyi noticed for the first time that there was no handle inside. Two hours passed before the door opened again. Alatren preceded a middle-aged woman in a dress that was too tight for her. She sat down, a stenographer's pad on her knee, looking everywhere but at Szechenyi.

Alatren perched on the side of the table. "The first thing I want you to do is relax. I told you, this is just a formality, but it has to be done. I'm going to ask the questions. You will supply the answers. The señora does the hard work. It's all perfectly straightforward."

Szechenyi hesitated. The effects of the brandy had worn off already. "Should I not see a lawyer?"

Alatren touched his bald spot with the delicacy of a mosquito alighting.

"A *lawyer?*" he repeated. "I don't think you understand, Señor Szechenyi. I said this is purely routine. You don't need a lawyer. The medical examiner has already released your son's body for burial. We'll give you a release. I'm sorry you have been kept for so long."

Szechenyi raised his head, fearing a trap of some kind. "Whatever you ask, I will answer, señor."

The police-captain's questions were a repetition of what he had asked before. Szechenyi's statement covered four pages of the stenographer's pad.

"As soon as you can," Alatren said to the woman. "Señor Szechenyi is in a hurry to leave us." His smile bound them in friendly complicity.

The stenographer was back in five minutes with the finished typescript. Szechenyi signed both copies and the woman left. Alatren took her chair, tapping a Ducado out of the pack. The room filled with the strong, sweet smell of black tobacco.

"This is off the record now," Alatren said confidentially. "Do you own an ice-pick?"

Szechenyi nodded. "There is one in the kitchen drawer. Or was."

"Can you remember when you last saw it?"

Szechenyi searched his memory and failed. "I have no idea."

Alatren leaned forward. "An ice-pick was found in the car-park under your son's bedroom window. It is the weapon he was killed with."

Szechenyi gave his attention to picking at a stain on his jacket.

"He was stabbed while asleep," said Alatren. "And drunk. You can forget what you've read, señor. Victims of heart wounds do *not* always die immediately! They can be conscious and able for some time, anything up to ten seconds, long enough for your son to move from the bed to where you found him. The murderer dropped the ice-pick from the window and left the way he came. If it *is* a he, that is."

Szechenyi brought his voice under control. "You mean it could be a woman?"

"That's right," said Alatren. "The lock on your front door is a joke. One of my men opened it with a credit card. Let me ask you something, Señor Szechenyi. Just how close were you to your son?"

Memories took shape. The bitter arguments, most of them about money, the grudging collaboration that hid Karolyi's resentment.

"It hasn't been easy," he admitted. "It is difficult for my children to see things as I do. It isn't the difference in age alone. I am Hungarian. My children are Spanish. There are problems."

Alatren opened his palm, letting a book of paper matches

fall on the table. The name "Bar Pasapogo" was printed on the cover.

"Do you know this place?"

Neither name nor address meant anything. "No," said Szechenyi. He waited for what came next.

"I didn't think that you would," Alatren said easily. "It is a bar used by high-class whores." He opened the matchbook cover. Someone had blocked out a telephone number with an eyebrow pencil. "These matches were found in your son's clothing. He was in the Bar Pasapogo last night. He arrived just after ten o'clock, drank a couple of Cuba libres and called this number. It belongs to a German student, Inge Grunelius. The lady supplements her income with prostitution."

Szechenyi drew a sharp breath. "I do not believe it!"

"Why not?" Alatren dropped the matches in his shirt pocket. "Maybe you didn't know your son as well as you thought you did. This woman joined him in the Bar Pasapogo. They had a meal there and left together. We have found the cabdriver who drove them to the woman's apartment. He has already identified your son's body. Karolyi left the apartment at one o'clock this morning. We haven't found the second cabdriver but rest assured that we will."

"I'm not sure that I understand," said Szechenyi. "You think this woman killed Karolyi?" It was difficult to eliminate Gotsek from his mind.

"It's a possibility," said Alatren, pitching his cigarette through the window. "A woman may well have done it, according to the medical examiner. Death occurred between five and seven this morning. It is difficult to be more precise in this heat. The problem is that the girl claims that she never left her flat after she went home with your son. It seems that another man visited her later. According to her, he was there until ten o'clock this morning. She's downstairs now. We're checking her story."

Szechenyi's stomach churned. He had refused the food on

the plane and it was ten hours since he had eaten. His mind still chased Gotsek.

"What about this other man she was with?"

Alatren looked away. "All we have is a description. These people don't give their right names. The woman claims that he got her number from the barman at the Pasapogo. We're checking that too."

A fresh note crept into the policeman's voice. It was almost one of respect. "There is something you omitted to tell me, Señor Szechenyi. Something that might give us the motive we're looking for. It seems that you're a very rich man."

Szechenyi cleared his throat. *The documents from the bank were in his flight bag.*

"I'm not rich, señor. The money does not belong to me. This is what I had to explain to my children. I had already talked things over with my daughter. I intended to tell my son today."

"You mean that neither of them knew about it?" Alatren's face was incredulous.

Szechenyi smiled sadly. "The one thing I am good at is keeping a secret. I have had forty years practice."

Alatren spoke as if something else was on his mind. "You've had a fascinating life, Señor Szechenyi. I borrowed your file from the Ministry of Justice. It's odd, but I was a flyer too. I did my military service in the Air Force. Where will you sleep tonight? Have you friends in the city you can stay with?"

Szechenyi passed his hand across his wet forehead. "Does that mean I can go?"

"Of course you can go!" Alatren's sun-tanned face was solicitous. "You are free to go whenever you wish. All I need to know is where I can find you."

Szechenyi scribbled a telephone number and pulled himself up with an effort. "Thank you for your consideration. You have been kind."

"I am a father too," said Alatren. "Two girls, eleven and nine. I'll take you down to the office. You'll need an authorization to claim your son's body from the morgue. And there's your passport and bag."

The hand on Szechenyi's arm offered friendly support as the two men walked down the cloisters. The cobble-stones outside were wet with the spray from the fountain. Szechenyi carried his bag to the street, his muscles reluctant to respond. A cab let him off near Atocha. He walked into the railroad station and used a phone booth.

"I've just left the police station. I think it's all right."

"Thank God for that," said Ilona.

"The police think you're in Portugal. Your brother was killed with an ice-pick."

A moment of shocked silence followed. "Do they know who did it?"

"The police are holding a German girl. Karolyi was with her last night." It was as much as he could bring himself to explain.

"And Gotsek?"

He glanced through the glass of the booth instinctively. "Not a word," he said. "Is John there?"

"Yes. Do you want to speak to him?"

"It doesn't matter. Do you remember Father Joseph?"

"Of course I remember," she answered quickly.

"I want you both to meet me there at eight o'clock. Be sure you're not followed."

He used the underpass and climbed the stairs to his office. The ascent seemed much steeper. A strong sense of guilt afflicted him, everything that he did somehow culpable. The office was as it had been left the night before. The alpaca jacket that Karolyi wore at work was hanging on the back of the door, the August catalogues on his desk ready for mailing.

Szechenyi had spent a large part of his life in this room with its horsehair sofa and moth-eaten carpet. A stained, enamelled coffee-pot perched on top of the old-fashioned safe. A few philatelic reference books were arranged on a bookcase. A giant fan with blades like an airplane propeller was set in the ceiling. Szechenyi opened his son's desk with misgiving. He had always respected his children's privacy. The drawers were unlocked. No attempt had been made to conceal their contents. He sat sad-faced, leafing through the pile of papers. Travel brochures: Acapulco for the Discerning, Buy/Rent a Château in the Dordognes, Cruise the Caribbean. There was a coloured photograph of a Ferrari GT4 clipped to a typewritten sheet of specifications. *Metallic red with black velour trim, air-conditioned, wide wheels, every conceivable extra.*

He dropped the items in the trash-basket one by one. The letter demanding payment for a bill incurred in a restaurant. A confirmation certificate. Notes on a stamp-collection being offered for sale. Szechenyi added the unmailed catalogues to the junk in the basket. It was he who had failed his children, not the other way round.

He started as the telephone rang in front of him. Gotsek's voice was loud in his ear.

"I am sitting across the street in the Alemán. Join me."

Szechenyi hurried to the mirror in time to see the blue-flannelled figure emerge from the restaurant and resume his seat at Szechenyi's usual sidewalk table. Szechenyi let the curtain fall. There was no escape. He walked down the stairs and out into the cacophony of the evening traffic. Gotsek slipped a marker in the book he was reading. A glass of brandy was waiting in front of the empty seat. His freckled face was sympathetic.

"I heard the news. I am sorry."

Szechenyi's first attempt to raise the glass failed. He tried again, using both hands. Noise roared in his head. He looked across the table, imagining himself aiming a gun at Gotsek's head. His accusation was bitter.

"You killed my son!"

Gotsek shook his head. "You are out of your mind, my friend. I assure you I know nothing of Karolyi's death."

Szechenyi lowered the empty glass. "Why are you here in Madrid?"

A hint of exasperation showed in Gotsek's face. "I wouldn't be here if you hadn't left Portugal. You're putting your trust in the wrong people."

Szechenyi locked his fingers together to keep them from shaking. "What do you mean by that?"

Gold fillings flashed as Gotsek smiled. "Come on, now, you know very well what I mean. You're playing a dangerous game, my friend." He spoke like a man who is sure of his facts.

It was difficult for Szechenyi to answer. "This is no game. My son has been murdered."

Gotsek's finger-nails rattled the top of the table. "The Englishman, the man I saw at the villa. How much does he know?"

"Nothing!" The lie was spoken with confidence.

"The villa is empty," said Gotsek smoothly. "Your daughter is not at her office. Where are they?"

"They drove to the Algarve last night. The Englishman wanted to look at some property."

"I hope you're not lying," said Gotsek. He pushed his coffee-cup aside. "Why did you stay? Your son came back yesterday."

The brandy provided a measure of courage. "I needed to talk to my daughter. Don't you understand, for God's sake? I had to explain your visit. The Englishman thinks that you're just a friend. I told Ilona the truth in private. She agreed that it involved the family. She wanted me to talk to Karolyi."

Gotsek's sandy eyelashes fluttered. "The police are holding a woman on suspicion of murdering him. A German called Inge Grunelius. The officer in charge is a Captain Alatren. Do you want me to continue?"

"I have kept faith with you," Szechenyi muttered.

"I hope so." Gotsek pursed his lips, probing the truth. "You have to face facts. Regrettable though it is, your son's death changes nothing. The terms of my offer remain unaltered."

"I need time," Szechenyi said obstinately.

Gotsek brought his fist down on the table. "Listen to me very carefully. *I* am the only real friend that you have. I am gambling my reputation on your making the right decision, and by God you had better make it! If not, it's the end of you and your daughter. If you've any sense left, you will know I'm not bluffing."

He pushed an envelope across the table. "This is a transfer-form from your bank. All it needs is the number of your account and the signature. We'll do the rest. Where are you sleeping tonight?"

"With friends. The funeral is being held tomorrow morning."

"And then?"

"I'm taking the afternoon plane back to Lisbon."

"Put this in your pocket," said Gotsek, tapping the envelope.

Szechenyi obeyed. "I shall have to talk to the bank."

Gotsek consulted his watch. "There has been too much talk already. All that is necessary is for you to complete the transfer. You have until noon on Sunday."

He picked up his panama hat, the benevolent look back on his face. "I'll see you in Portugal—and remember, there is no place to hide."

He raised his hat with a courteous gesture and was lost among the window-shoppers thronging the pavement. His cigarette continued to burn in the ashtray.

Szechenyi ground it to shreds and walked back to the dingy office. He unlocked the safe and added its contents to the contents of the trash-basket. He sat at the empty desk, looking round the room. His break with the past was deliberate. Once he left Spain, he would never return. Whatever else lay in store, that much was certain.

Somebody knocked and the door was pushed open. A middle-aged man in black came in hugging a sample case against his chest.

"Señor Szechenyi? I am Diego Cruz."

Szechenyi indicated the empty seat.

Cruz lowered himself carefully. "Father Sallai informed me. You have our deepest condolences." He opened his sample case with the delicacy of a bomb-disposal expert.

"You are able to take charge of everything?" asked Szechenyi.

Cruz nodded, his manner discreet. "You will find that our work is carried out with taste and reverence, señor." He spread a collection of black-and-white photographs across the desk for Szechenyi's inspection. The glossy prints were of coffins and headstones. The undertaker licked a finger, displaying a picture of a free-form angel soaring from a black marble crypt.

Szechenyi's face thinned with disgust. "No! Everything must be as simple as possible."

Cruz whipped away all but one of the photographs. "Then this is what the gentleman needs," he said unctuously. "We call it our Cavalry model. For a headstone in a similar price-range we recommend granite. The stone is less expensive than marble and it weathers better."

Szechenyi kept rein on his repugnance. "This is the inscription I want."

Cruz read aloud from the piece of paper. "Karolyi Szechenyi. Born October 6, 1958. Murdered July 19, 1983." He made a noise in his throat. "I am not sure that the church authorities . . ."

Szechenyi cut him short. "You provide the coffin and headstone. I will take care of the church authorities. The funeral is at eleven o'clock tomorrow morning in the parish church of Rincón de la Victoria. Father Sallai will conduct the service. There will be no flowers and no cortège. Is all that quite clear?"

Cruz bowed his head. "We pride ourselves on meeting the wishes of our bereaved ones, señor. I understand that the remains are with the police?"

Szechenyi gave the official release to the undertaker. "The body is in the morgue. Eleven o'clock, and bring your bill with you."

He closed the door on the undertaker and locked it for the last time, leaving a card tacked on it bearing his lawyer's name and address.

Dust rose and settled on the cactus plants that bordered the road. The cab jolted over the humpbacked bridge. The village in front of them clung to the side of the mountain. A church belfry soared against the sky a couple of hundred feet above the huddle of houses below.

The cabdriver stopped on the unpaved square and switched off the motor. Women were sitting in doorways, weaving rushes into baskets. Children played among browsing donkeys. Layers of whitewash caked the adobe shacks. The only buildings of importance were the church, presbytery and school.

The cabdriver spat into the dust, dislodging a small green lizard. "I hope you are only visiting."

Nothing had changed since Szechenyi's last visit. The same tired fruit and vegetables were displayed outside the *tienda*, the same bead curtain protected the interior from the swarms of bugs that sought entrance.

It was after seven o'clock, but the sun was still hot. The women suspended their work, watching as Szechenyi crossed the square to the zigzag of steps that was cut in the rock. There were fifty in all, worn by countless feet and ending in a shady courtyard between the church and the presbytery.

Szechenyi climbed slowly, husbanding his breath. The smell of incense drifted down from the church above. He put his bag down at the top of the steps and pulled on a rope. A bell jangled inside the presbytery. The sun-blistered door was opened by a priest wearing a silk bombazine soutane and black buckled shoes.

The priest folded Szechenyi in a wordless embrace and took his bag. The two men were roughly the same age, but Sallai looked ten years younger. He led the way up a staircase smelling of beeswax. The room he opened contained a small single bed. A crucifix hung above the pillow, a framed map of pre-war Hungary at its side.

Father Sallai put Szechenyi's bag on the bed, almost losing his eyes in the width of his smile.

"I believe it is time for a drink," he said in Hungarian, rubbing his hands together.

The parlour was cheerful with chintz-covered chairs and sofa. Rugs were strewn across the polished floor. The bookshelves were well stocked. Standing by the window was a life-size statue of St. Francis of Assisi, the carved wood painted and gilded. A vast open fireplace heated the room in winter. Father Sallai held a bottle of sherry to the light before filling two glasses.

Szechenyi touched his lips to the drink and sat down, thinking of the night of Hungary's total surrender. The memory endured in detail; the embassy staff assembled in the ballroom, the ambassador in full diplomatic uniform, his voice close to tears as he broke the news to his stunned audience. The fight was over, he said, their futures a matter for their consciences.

He himself was returning to Budapest. The scene closed with an emotional singing of the national anthem. Sallai had been embassy chaplain. Three men and one woman had left

Spain with the ambassador. None survived their return to Hungary. Those who stayed on in Madrid drifted away one by one during the days that followed until only Sallai and Szechenyi were left. They lasted for eleven weeks, burning candles when the power was cut off, using furniture as fuel in the bitter winter weather. When the news came of Admiral Horthy's arrest, the two men left the embassy by way of the front gates, Sallai in his cloak and biretta, Szechenyi wearing the uniform of the Royal Hungarian Air Force. He surrendered the embassy keys to the Swiss chargé d'affaires, shook Sallai's hand and went his own way. When they met again, seven years later, Sallai was a parish priest in Murcia, Szechenyi married and living in the same apartment he lived in now.

The priest rammed a pinch of snuff into each nostril and blew into a tissue. "Cruz telephoned half an hour ago. They have cut the stone. They're sending it up tonight. It will only be a short requiem. In Latin, of course."

Szechenyi nodded. His friend's loyalty was beyond question, but it had been impossible for Szechenyi to confide in him. The secret he had carried for so long seemed to have poisoned his closest relationships.

"I would like to give some money to the church," he said impulsively. "I shall soon be in a position to do so."

"As a priest, I am grateful," smiled Sallai. "As a friend, I advise some reflection. Once we have it in our clutches, money is hard to regain." He glanced at his watch. "I'm leaving you alone in the house. My housekeeper is at her sister's and I must hear confession. God help me, Stephen, there is one poor soul with the breath of a fish-hawk. I have thought seriously of wearing a gas mask." The priest's attempt to remain cheerful was obvious.

"You're a good friend," Szechenyi said gratefully.

Sallai shook his head. "It's a bad business, but with God's help you'll survive it. Give my love to Ilona."

It was some time before the Volkswagen came into view,

clattering over the bridge across the arroyo. Szechenyi stationed himself at the top of the steps. There was a clear view along the valley as far as the next village. Nothing was following the Volkswagen. Dust rose as it turned into the square below. Ilona was out first, Raven close behind her. They shaded their eyes, looking up at the presbytery. Szechenyi waved and they began to climb. He hurried them into the house and took his daughter in his arms. Her body was stiff and unresponsive. Raven shrugged. It was clear that the strain was beginning to tell on all of them.

"What's the matter?" Szechenyi said gently.

Ilona shook herself free, her long hair escaping its pinning. "I don't know how you can ask me that! My brother's dead and I can't even see him buried. That's what you've done to us!"

The outburst was totally unexpected. A couple of seconds elapsed before its impact registered. Szechenyi swung his hand without thinking, his palm catching her flush on the side of the face. It was the first time in his life that he had struck her in this way. His voice shook with shame and resentment.

"Never say a thing like that again!" he warned.

She touched her cheek with her fingertips, looking from them to her father. They continued to stare at one another in silence. Ilona broke first, burying her face against Szechenyi's chest. He pulled the dirty handkerchief from his pocket and wiped her eyes tenderly.

"It's going to be all right," he soothed. "Everything's going to be all right."

He wrapped an arm around her shoulders and led her into the kitchen. It was a big room with an old-fashioned wood-stove. A smoked ham hung from a hook in the yellowed ceiling. An open bottle of red wine and glasses stood on the table in the last of the sunshine. Copper pans gleamed on the dresser. Raven was at the window, doing his best to hide his embarrassment.

"I'm sorry," Szechenyi said awkwardly. The apology was for both of them. "I don't know what came over me."

Raven filled the wineglasses. "It's Ilona who should be apologizing."

Her face was still red from the force of the blow. "If that's meant to be a rebuke, maybe I should remind you that it is none of your business."

"You're right," he replied. "I shouldn't be here in the first place."

"For God's sake!" said Szechenyi. "What's happening to us?" The other two eyed one another warily. "We're alone in the house," he continued. "Let's sit down and talk sense."

Raven's face cleared. "It's about time someone started talking sense; I am beginning to run out of patience."

Szechenyi pushed a glass in his daughter's direction. "Gotsek is here in Madrid. I saw him a couple of hours ago. He swears he had nothing to do with Karolyi's death."

"What did you expect him to say?" Ilona's look was stony.

Raven whipped a chair under his buttocks. "Lisbon yesterday, Madrid today. I'd have thought that spoke for itself."

"He's made that quite clear," said Szechenyi. "He says that he followed me. We have until noon on Sunday."

A bell started to toll in the church. Raven closed the window. "You mean you're still going ahead with this business?"

Szechenyi closed his ears to the doleful stroke of the bell. "I believe Gotsek. I don't think he's responsible."

His daughter turned to Raven. "Do you believe that?"

He emptied his glass reflectively. "There's an expression in English about biting off more than you can chew. That's what I think we're doing."

Ilona's smile was wry. "What he's trying to say is that he'd like to go home. He's too squeamish to be honest."

Raven's jaw firmed. "Don't put words in my mouth. I meant what I said. But things are getting out of hand and there's a limit to what I'm prepared to do. It's time to be frank with each other. I take it you've made your decision?"

Szechenyi moistened his lips as the other two hung on his answer.

"I've made my decision. Gotsek brought all that is necessary. There is no alternative. I'm taking his offer."

His daughter closed her eyes. "Thank God for that."

"Does Gotsek know this?" said Raven.

Szechenyi moved his head in assent. "We are meeting in Lisbon. There are arrangements that have to be made."

Raven opened the window again. The bell had stopped ringing. "What about the police? They may not like the idea of your leaving."

Szechenyi refilled his glass. "They'll let me go," he said with confidence. "Alatren understands. He's treated me like a human being."

Raven rolled his eyes at the ceiling. "That does it! Any time a cop treats you like a human being, you ask for the cards to be reshuffled. I speak from experience. Does he know where you are right now, for example?"

Szechenyi looked at him defensively. "He knows that I'm with friends. I gave him the number."

Raven reversed his chair and straddled it. "Then be sure that he'll be at the funeral. Don't they have inquests in Spain?"

"Not if the cause of death is established."

Raven gave the answer some thought. "Did Alatren give *you* a number to call?"

"Two," said Szechenyi. "His home and the office."

Raven brooded again. "There's one thing that sticks out a mile in my mind. The sooner we're all back in Portugal, the better it's going to be. Agreed?"

Szechenyi nodded cautiously, sensing the tension between his daughter and Raven. It was almost one of antagonism.

"Let's have no misconceptions about what I'm saying,"

Raven said warningly. "I'm giving you people the same deadline as Gotsek. Noon on Sunday. After that you're on your own. I hope that's clear."

It was hard for Szechenyi to express the surge of relief he experienced. "I will not forget all that you have done, John."

There was a hint of self-mockery in Raven's reply. "I hope I don't live to regret it. The thing for you to do now is to call Alatren. Tell him you need to go back to your daughter. At least we'll know then how we stand."

Szechenyi pulled himself up. The phone was on the desk in the parlour. He dialled Alatren's home number and gave his name. The police-captain's voice was unsurprised.

"Señor Szechenyi! What can I do for you?"

Szechenyi cleared his throat. "I am staying the night with friends, as I told you, Captain. In Rincón de la Victoria."

"A wise choice. Is that all?"

A whiff of incense had found its mysterious way from the church. Szechenyi took the plunge.

"I am worried about my daughter."

The drawn-out sound in the policeman's throat covered a range of nuances. "Have you talked with her?"

Danger warned like a ticking time bomb. "She is in the Algarve with a friend. The girl Ilona works with expects her back tomorrow. My place is with my daughter, Captain. She needs me."

"Of course, I can understand." The response was courteous, even kindly, but it offered no real encouragement.

Szechenyi summoned his courage. "There is a plane for Lisbon at a quarter past two."

"And you'd like to be on it. Have you made a reservation yet?"

"I wanted to ask you first."

"I see no difficulty," Alatren answered. "Call me back if you have any difficulty. I have friends at Iberia. I shall see you in the morning in any case. Good night, Señor Szechenyi!"

Szechenyi went back to the kitchen. He wiped his mouth and reached for the bottle. There was an odd air of complicity about the other two now. He guessed that they had been talking about him.

"You were right," he said to Raven. "He's coming to the funeral."

"I'd be surprised if he didn't," said Raven.

The wine slopped down the front of Szechenyi's jacket. "I told him that Ilona was in the Algarve with a friend." He dabbed at his clothes with his handkerchief.

Raven's face tightened. "For God's sake, pull yourself together, man! Is he letting you leave the country or not?"

Szechenyi pushed the half-full glass to one side. "He even offered to get me a seat on the plane."

Ilona reached for her shoulder-bag. "Papa, we have to go!"

Szechenyi's hand stopped her. He felt in his pocket, showing her the ring he had removed from the safe in his office.

"I want you to take this with you. And not a word of it to anyone!"

She looked at the tarnished signet-ring, her eyes curious as she recognized the arms engraved on it. She slipped the ring in her bag and put her arms around her father.

"There's something I want you to know. I love you. No matter what happens, wherever you go, I'll be there. Remember that!"

His tears made a blur of her face, but at last he was purged of the guilt that oppressed him. What mattered now was to give her the happiness that she deserved.

"I'll be with you tomorrow," he promised. "I'll call you from the airport. Take care of her, John."

Raven picked up his cigarettes. "We should be in Beja by

midnight. Try to stay off the drink. You'll need all your wits
in the morning."

They walked to the top of the steps. Women were leaving
the church in the fading daylight, their heads covered in
the old-fashioned way. He watched the Volkswagen until its
tail-lights died in the distance.

CHAPTER 7

The telephone rang on the bedside-table. Gotsek reached across and turned off the radio. The desk clerk's voice fluted into the ear-piece.

"The gentleman you were expecting is here, señor."

"Send him up," said Gotsek. He slipped a few things into his travelling-bag. A bottle of Chivas Regal, his silver-backed hairbrushes, the calfskin folder containing his sheet music. All would offend his visitor's sense of propriety.

Somebody tapped on the door.

"Come!" Gotsek called in Hungarian. He moved forward, locking the practised smile into place.

His visitor was a man dressed in dark-grey clothing. A long nose and slightly protruding teeth gave him the appearance of a rat in gold-rimmed spectacles. He glanced round the room ironically.

"Still travelling in style, I see."

Gotsek's hand hovered above the bell-push. "May I offer you something to drink, Comrade Solti?"

Solti took a seat at the ornate Empire writing-desk. "There is no time to waste," he said curtly. "I can think of better things to do than spend two hours in this heat. Why couldn't you come to the airport?"

"I had things to do," Gotsek said easily. "I regret the inconvenience."

Solti's official position was that of a ministry messenger, a courier who collected diplomatic bags from the embassies. Like Gotsek, he held top-security clearance. He was also an agent of the KS.

Gotsek placed a sealed envelope on the desk. "My report."

Solti put the envelope in an inside pocket. His eyes, diminished by the thickness of his spectacle lens, were the size of bilberries.

"I would say you were in trouble, Counselor." The reflection gave him obvious pleasure.

Gotsek's gold fillings glinted as he smiled. "Wishful thinking, Comrade Solti. No more than wishful thinking."

Solti's arrival in Madrid was the response to Gotsek's urgent message. His selection was ominous. Solti shook his head, spurning Gotsek's offer of a cigarette. It was typical of the man that he smoked the cheapest Hungarian brand. He lit one now.

"I have a confession to make. I was surprised when I heard of your assignment."

"So I gathered," said Gotsek. Solti was a long-standing opponent of Gotsek's delicate approach.

Solti harnessed his fingers to his smoke and inhaled. "You will understand, there is nothing personal about my attitude. Your record speaks for itself, Counselor. I just happened to think that you were the wrong man for this particular mission. Events would appear to have proven me right."

Gotsek kept brakes on his temper. "That is pure nonsense."

"No!" Solti tilted the desk lamp so that his face was in shadow. "The son is killed and the police are involved! So much for the Gotsek approach."

There was a limit to how much Gotsek was prepared to take from his visitor.

"I have known you for nine years, Comrade Solti. I did not like you when I first met you. I still do not like you. Your function is to deliver the report I have given you."

Solti worried his teeth with his lips, producing a kind of smile.

"I believe you play chess. A finalist in the National Junior Championships, no less. The game is supposed to refine one's thinking."

"A losing finalist," Gotsek remembered. "You will not wish to miss your flight."

A police siren sounded on the street below. Neither man showed any sign of hearing it.

"I had forgotten," said Solti. "A *losing* finalist."

The buttons were off the foils, but Gotsek was sure of himself. "Let me tell you something to think about on your voyage home," he said, leaning forward. "Karolyi's death was pure coincidence. A woman has already been taken into custody."

Solti made no secret of his own hostility. "You will find a signal waiting for you in Lisbon, Counselor. The deadline will *not* be extended. It is something that you in turn may reflect on. I have a feeling that we will be seeing a lot more of one another. In Budapest," he added significantly.

Gotsek came to his feet. "I am glad that we had this talk. Let me wish you a safe journey home. Goodbye!"

He watched from the balcony as Solti scuttled into a cab. Gotsek lifted the telephone. It was a while before the Lisbon number replied.

"I have been trying to reach you all day," said Nylasi.

"I'm in Madrid," said Gotsek. "I'll be back tonight. Have Ottilio meet me at the airport."

"Ottilio?" Nylasi's surprise was evident.

"The plane arrives at a quarter to midnight. My car is a green Fiat. He will find it in the short-term car-park. If the plane is late, he must wait. He's taking his orders from me from now on." His authority still held, for the moment at least.

The Madrid–Lisbon shuttle landed on time. Gotsek's diplomatic passport took him quickly through customs. In spite of the late hour, the main hall was still crowded. Gotsek made his way outside to the car-park. Ottilio appeared from the shadows, still wearing the tight jeans and black leather jacket.

He lifted a hand in salute and climbed into the Fiat beside Gotsek.

"Where is your machine?" asked Gotsek.

Ottilio nodded. A Honda was propped against the wire fence fifteen yards away. The handlebars were hung with rabbit tails. A sleeping bag was tied to the pillion.

Gotsek felt for his cigarettes. "Can you do without sleep?" The answer was probably yes, but he had to be sure.

Ottilio's breath was loaded with garlic. "That depends upon the circumstances," he replied.

"What did Nylasi tell you tonight?"

Ottilio moved his shoulders. "That I had to meet you here, that I'd get my instructions from you."

There was a directness about the man that encouraged Gotsek. "How many of these people at the villa do you know by sight?"

"All five of them," said the Portuguese.

"There are only four," replied Gotsek. "The son is dead."

A shrug was the extent of Ottilio's interest. "The place has been empty all day."

"I need your help," Gotsek said frankly. "The house won't be empty for long. I have to know who leaves and when, if anyone you don't already know arrives."

"You mean you want me to camp there?"

"That's right," said Gotsek. "For the next couple of days. Do you think you could do that?"

Ottilio leaned forward until his forehead rested against the dash. Then he straightened up again.

"I can take food and a thermos of coffee. I've done it before."

"It's important that nobody sees you," urged Gotsek. "They may be expecting it."

Ottilio picked at his dirty finger-nails. "Nobody sees me when I don't want them to, sir. I'm good at my job."

"How have you been making your reports up to now?"

"It depends on the director. Sometimes we talk on the phone. Sometimes he wants to see me. It depends."

"Where is the nearest phone to the villa?"

Ottilio found the gold stud in his left ear. "The nearest I've found is on the outskirts of Sintra. But I don't like using it. There are too many people around. There's a better place on the other side of town."

Gotsek had the piece of paper ready. "This is where I'm staying. Call me at midnight tomorrow."

Szechenyi woke with a start from a dreamless sleep, disturbed by the banging on the bedroom door. The priest's voice was hearty.

"It's a quarter to eight! Breakfast in half an hour!"

Szechenyi emerged from the tangle of sheets and blankets. Sallai and he had talked until late, sitting in the sage-purple darkness. The conversation had been one between old friends, the silences as meaningful as the speech.

Szechenyi scratched himself vigorously and went into the bathroom. Ten minutes later he was carrying his bag down the stairs. The parlour blazed with freshly picked zinnias. The floor had been waxed and polished, the table in front of the window set for breakfast. There was an air of comfort and order that Szechenyi had missed for too long. The aroma of coffee drifted across from the kitchen.

He sat down at the desk and dialled the Vila Verde. His breathing quickened as he heard his daughter's voice. She sounded relaxed.

"Everything's fine at this end. We had a clear run through, no problems at all at the frontier. Did you get your seat booked?"

"They confirmed it last night," he replied. "We're due at Portela at twenty to four. Is John there with you?"

"Yes, he's here," she said.

He found her cavalier manner offensive. "I'd like you to show a little more gratitude," he said. "John is a true friend."

"I know it," she said indifferently. "Look, I'm in a rush to get to the office. I'll pick you up at the airport."

He was still sitting at the desk when the priest came in followed by a grey-haired woman in black. She placed a tray on the breakfast table, turning a melancholy look on Szechenyi before leaving the room. The priest smeared toast with butter, covered it with mountain honey, and shoved the coffee-pot across the table.

Szechenyi filled the blue bowl, shaking his head at the offer of food. "I'm not hungry."

"You said that last night!" The priest's eyebrows met disapprovingly. "The body requires to be fed no less than the soul!"

Szechenyi stared at him over the earthenware bowl. "I am in trouble, Joseph. It's nothing to do with Karolyi. It's something else."

"'A trouble shared . . .'" quoted the priest. "Do you want to talk about it?"

Szechenyi wavered, encouraged by the priest's compassion. Of all men, Sallai was the one he should have confided in.

"It isn't a question of trust, surely?" Sallai probed gently.

Szechenyi moved his head from side to side. "Do you know what it is to be afraid, Joseph? I mean *really* afraid!"

The answer came promptly. "As often as I examine my conscience."

"I don't mean that sort of fear," said Szechenyi. "I'm talking about the turmoil in your mind when someone you love is in danger."

"I have known that too," the priest said quietly. "Don't be fooled by this collar I'm wearing."

"I'm not," said Szechenyi. They had drunk together too

often in the old days for that to be possible, sitting surrounded by dust-sheeted furniture, the snow shifting on the roof of the embassy, the city gripped by relentless winter.

The priest clapped his hands together loudly and bawled. "More coffee, Señora Duarte!"

The housekeeper collected the uneaten food, vinegar-nosed with disapproval. She returned with a fresh pot of coffee, her expression still reproachful.

"How many people will there be for lunch, Señor Padre?" Her Andalusian accent swallowed the consonants.

"Only me," said Sallai. "One o'clock sharp and no goat!"

The housekeeper sailed across the hallway. Sallai closed the door behind her.

"If she were younger, prettier and more amiable, my reputation would suffer. As it is, she's a cross I must bear, albeit unwillingly."

Szechenyi drew a long breath and unburdened himself, hiding nothing.

"A terrible story," Sallai said. "You kept your secret well."

Szechenyi cradled the coffee bowl in both hands, trapped in the memory.

"Nobody knew," said the priest. "Not even the ambassador. I remember the rumours when you were recalled to Budapest. It wasn't until years later that I put two and two together. I was on a train. Someone had left a copy of a Swiss newspaper in the dining-car, and there it was, plastered all over the front page: 'Communists Lay Claim to Bank of Hungary Bullion.'"

It was a peaceful room with Saint Francis, the books and the flowers, an expression of faith both in God and humanity.

The priest leaned forward. "Can you support an old friend's honest opinion?"

"I ask for nothing better," Szechenyi said humbly.

"This Englishman is right. You should have gone to the authorities in the first place. Now it's too late. You have talked a great deal about honour and duty, but the plain truth is that money has almost destroyed you. Are you going to let it destroy your daughter as well?"

Szechenyi found his voice with difficulty. "Tell me what I must do, Joseph. She is all I have left."

"You will find no escape in others," the priest answered. "The decision must be yours. Come, let me show you where Karolyi will be buried."

The two men crossed the square, followed by the chanting of children in the school. The loose dirt had been raked and sprinkled with water. Sallai had a smile and a wave for whoever greeted him. Szechenyi quickened his pace, a sense of loneliness deepening his depression. The walled cemetery was three hundred yards from the village. It was a country cemetery with no great vaults or family mausoleums. The bulk of the graves were forgotten, the ground reclaimed by unkempt grass. Sallai stopped in front of a mound of newly dug earth. This was the highest point in the burial-ground. The headstone was already in place, the inscription lined with black. A six-foot-deep pit had been opened to receive the coffin. A couple of trestles and a rope lay on the mound of fresh earth.

Szechenyi turned his head, overcome by grief. His friend was bent over, weeding a nearby grave. The priest wiped his hands on his socks and straightened his back.

"You're out of condition," he said, snorting air into snuff-coated nostrils and flapping his arms. "You should take more exercise."

"You can be a hard man at times," said Szechenyi. Hornets droned near a hole in the wall, accentuating the stillness of the scene.

"I'm a friend," said Sallai. "There's a difference. All you have left are the years that remain and your daughter. I want you to make the most of them."

Back at the presbytery, they sat together at the parlour window, the priest reading yesterday's newspaper, bifocals low on his nose. Szechenyi's eyes followed the cloud of dust rising above the stubbled fields below.

"Here they come," he said nervously.

The two vehicles began the long ascent to the church, a Citroën hearse leading a black Seat. Sallai lowered his newspaper.

"You can leave the policeman to me. They still have respect for the cloth."

Lamps decorated the front of the hearse, forming a series of coloured crosses when lit. The coffin looked small through the plate-glass windows. Alatren swung himself out of the Seat and stretched his arms, looking round curiously. Szechenyi made the introductions.

The policeman's smile embraced them both. "You are certainly hidden away here, Father. I would never have found it had I not followed the hearse."

"I'm afraid we are very isolated," the priest said easily. "The military have to dig us out every winter."

Alatren settled himself on the low wall, arranging the creases in his trousers.

"Your Spanish is excellent, if you will allow me to say so, Father."

The pressure of Sallai's hand on Szechenyi's sleeve was reassuring.

"You mean for a foreigner. I am Hungarian too. Stephen and I are old friends."

The police-captain grinned ingenuously. "I know that, Father. I've been doing my homework. Señor Szechenyi was lucky to find you again after all this time."

"We never really lost one another." The priest was giving as good as he got.

Alatren came off the wall, brushing his jacket. "I make a point of attending funerals when I am concerned with the victim. It isn't just a mark of respect, it's something in my head. A sense of unfinished business, if you like. I am glad

that you managed to secure your reservation, Señor Szechenyi."

Szechenyi nodded. Alatren had clearly checked with the
airport. "I was hoping I might get a lift back to the city."

"No problem," Alatren said smoothly.

The bell had started to toll. The priest took Szechenyi's
arm again. A few elderly women and the housekeeper were
sitting in the pews in the side-chapel. Szechenyi knelt, burying his face in his hands as Sallai appeared with his acolyte.
The short mass ended with a plea for forgiveness and
mercy. Szechenyi crossed himself and followed the others
out into the brilliant sunshine. He drove to the cemetery in
Alatren's car. The hearse stopped at the gates, too wide to
enter. A couple of men lifted the coffin onto a wheelbarrow
and trundled it up the pathway, one pushing, the other
steadying the load. The small group of mourners assembled
at the side of the open grave. Sallai said a short prayer. The
ropes creaked and the coffin was lowered. Szechenyi slipped
away, unwilling to stay any longer. Part of his life had gone
with the coffin.

The driver of the hearse had brought the account. Szechenyi paid it and climbed back into Alatren's car. The
others came down the pathway, the priest leading. He took
Szechenyi's hands through the open window, speaking in
Hungarian.

"God be with you, Stephen, and remember, you can always count on me."

"I shall remember," Szechenyi said steadily.

The Seat rolled down the hill, the movement dislodging
some books in the glove compartment. Behind them was a
police-special .38.

"A tool of the trade," Alatren said amiably.

He drove with one hand on the wheel, gesticulating with
the other as he chatted along. He seemed to show great interest in Szechenyi's friendship with the priest. Szechenyi

answered warily. Their eyes occasionally met in the rear-view mirror.

There was no change at all in Alatren's tone. "Have you been completely frank with me?"

Alarm sounded through Szechenyi's nervous system. "I'm not quite sure what you mean," he replied.

"I think you are," said the detective. "Had I known that you were a very rich man it might have had some bearing on my investigations." From someone who had seemed prepared to offer sympathy, he had taken on the aspect of a prosecuting attorney.

They covered the next few miles in silence, Alatren making no concessions as he barrelled through a gypsy settlement where children, horses and dogs milled around among the battered campers and trucks.

Finally, the police-captain resumed the discussion. "We're still holding the German girl, but she is sticking to her story. We've been unable to trace the other man. I have to confess I don't like it."

Drops of cold sweat rolled down Szechenyi's rib-cage.

Alatren took his gaze from the road very briefly. "Let me put it this way, Señor Szechenyi. I like to think that I am good at my job, but I make the occasional mistake. In fact, there's a drawer in my desk that's a constant reminder of failure. Inquiries that came to nothing, cases unsolved for one or another reason. That sort of thing."

Szechenyi cleared his throat painfully. "Does that mean that we will never find out who killed Karolyi?"

Alatren flashed a sideways smile. "We'll know, señor. Sooner or later, we'll know. How long do you intend to stay in Portugal?"

Szechenyi stumbled through the answer. "I'm not quite sure. It depends on my daughter."

"No matter," said Alatren, lifting a hand on the wheel. "We can always get hold of you. There is one thing you should know, however. A report came through last night from a highway patrolman living in Florida, very close to your home, in fact. It seems that he was on his way to work early yesterday morning and saw this Volkswagen convertible parked near the Metro station. There was nobody in it. That and the fact that the plates were Portuguese made him curious. He took the numbers."

A block between Szechenyi's brain and his mouth made it impossible for him to speak. Alatren swung the Seat onto the slip-road that led to the airport and drew up in front of the terminal buildings. A uniformed cop loomed into view, recognized Alatren, saluted and went on his way. Alatren leaned back, smoke curling from the Ducado between his lips.

"I can do two things with that report, Señor Szechenyi. I can ask the frontier posts to check their records for movement of a Volkswagen convertible with Portuguese plates or I can simply put a match to the report. I would like you to think about it. Please don't do anything foolish. We have a very good working relationship with the Portuguese police."

CHAPTER 8

Raven climbed up from the beach, sucking ozone deep into his lungs. The sunshine was warm on his body and he was glad to be back in Portugal. They had taken turns driving, catnapping through the tortuous mountain roads, reaching the villa at half past two in the morning. He had heard Ilona moving about before six o'clock.

She appeared on the patio steps as he lifted himself up from the dunes. "Breakfast!" she called. She was wearing a yellow dress, with her mass of dark hair pinned up on her neck.

He followed her into the kitchen. "My father just called," she announced. "I'm collecting him from the airport. What are your movements likely to be?"

He pulled up a chair and sat down on it. "I've got a feeling that we're seeing too much of one another. I think I'll catch up on some sleep."

She was fixing eggs for scrambling, standing with her back to him. It was a moment before he realized that she was crying. He started to go towards her. She whipped round furiously as he neared, tears and mascara running down her cheeks.

"Don't touch me!" she warned. "Just keep away from me!"

He backed off, holding his hands up in front of him.

"Just eat your breakfast and leave me alone," she insisted. She slapped the scrambled eggs down on the table and got as far as the door. She changed her mind and came back, sitting down facing him.

"Don't you have any sort of feelings at all?" she demanded.

He looked at her for a while, clearing his palate of egg. "That sounds to me like a loaded question."

She dabbed at her mascara-stained cheeks, her eyes scornful. "You make me sick. I'm going to tell you something about yourself, John Raven. You're going to end up a sad and lonely man. You have a problem. You can't give and you're incapable of taking."

He wiped his mouth, uncomfortable under the attack and ignorant of its purpose. He gained time, taking his plate to the sink and running hot water over it. He lit a couple of cigarettes and passed one to her.

She accepted it resentfully, her gaze half-veiled. "Have you decided what you're going to tell Kirstie?"

"About what?" He already knew the answer.

"About us."

A depth-charge sank in his brain and exploded. "There isn't any 'us'! I thought we'd made that quite clear."

She clenched her fists, the knuckles bone white. "There are some things that cannot be forgotten that easily."

"Wrong," he replied. "The kind of thing that you have in mind is all too easily forgotten."

Her eyebrows made twin sable lines. "I suppose that I should have known," she said heavily.

"Should have known *what?*" he cried. "Look, Ilona. We're two human beings. There are reasons for what happened yesterday, but they just don't apply any more. All that's over, finished!"

"Just like that?" she bit off each word.

"Just like that," he parroted. "Anything else would be stupid for both of us."

She veiled her eyes again, blowing a stream of smoke. "For a happily married man especially. You *are* a happily married man, aren't you?"

"Yes," he said. It took a fraction of a second longer to answer than it should have done.

The unexpectedness of her venom made its onslaught all the more shocking. "I *hate* that woman! I hated her at school and I hate her now! Whatever I wanted, she always had it. Do you know what it's like to be poor at a school for the children of the rich? *Do* you? Have you any idea how cruel they can be, girls of that age, your own sweet wife included?"

"That's crap," he said. "And I'm glad she's not sitting here listening to it. She's your friend, for crissakes, a woman who'd run her veins straight into yours if she had to."

"I'll bet," she said bitterly. "But don't worry, you're safe enough. Whatever happened between us, whatever was said, I'll bide my time."

"You missed your vocation," he answered. "You should have been an actress." Maybe it was the drugs she still took that gave her this obsession with drama.

"Is that the end of the conversation?" he asked. She was standing at the sink, putting the plates in the drying-rack.

She swung round, her face suddenly wiped clean of antagonism. "I'm not really the bitch you seem to think I am. It's a pity that I'll never have the chance now to prove it."

"The chance is just what you *do* have," he told her. "No matter how you feel, Kirstie is still your friend. For God's sake, keep her out of all this."

She gave him one of her secret smiles. "I told you, you're safe. Don't worry. I can't expect you to understand, but I love her as much as I hate her."

He changed the subject deliberately. "What are you going to do, go straight from here to the airport?"

Like him, she seemed ready to avoid more unpleasantness. "I have to go to the office. There are things to be taken care of."

He ran a film in his mind of Kirstie's face as he tried to

explain the events of the past few hours. She liked her emotions uncomplicated. There was no such colour as grey in her scheme of things. The division between white and black was arbitrary. He was fully aware that she saw him as a catalyst for disaster, a man impelled by a perverse wish to destroy himself. He had a quick urge to run from this house, to take the first plane home.

"You can't go on like this," he said impulsively. "What are you going to do with your life?"

"I'll go on like this to the end of my days," she said bitterly. "Following my father, defending him right or wrong. A dutiful daughter."

"And afterwards?"

She repeated the question aloud to herself. "You don't know the kind of man my father is. Nobody knows except me. All these things he talks about—family, honour, tradition—they're like the drugs I take. Just something to keep reality at bay. The terrifying thing is that he can't face the truth about himself."

"Few of us can," shrugged Raven. "Most of the time it's an unpleasant sight."

She sat down again, her eyes steady behind the screen of tobacco smoke. "Can we still talk as friends?"

"What else?" he replied.

She brushed through the smoke to see him more clearly. "We're talking about the truth, John. Gotsek knows my father for what he really is, an old, weak man who's a failure. A man incapable of making a decision for himself. That's why his hand must always be forced. That's why Karolyi was murdered."

It was a stark assessment of someone you loved, but part of it was probably true.

"You still think Gotsek's responsible?"

"I'm sure of it," she said with decision. "No matter how, he was behind Karol ʋ 's murder."

Raven kept his disagreement to himself. "You matter

more to your father than anything else," he said. "A lot of dreams are going to come true for both of you. Take my word for it!"

"It's too late for my dreams to come true," she said sadly. She seemed bent upon a new explanation. "A lot of what I said I didn't mean."

He grinned. "Now that's a bad trait. It can get you into a whole lot of trouble."

She reached across the table, taking his two hands in hers. "She doesn't deserve you. I do."

Once she had gone, he stretched out on the recliner, thinking that most of the real problems he had had in his life had been caused by women. Ilona Szechenyi was an example. His apprehension of her behaviour was growing. No matter what she said now, her earlier threats had been made in earnest and she'd have to be watched.

His toe-nails caught his attention. They needed cutting. He remembered seeing a pair of nail-clippers in Ilona's bedroom. They were in a tray on the dressing-table, next to Szechenyi's signet-ring. He took the ring to the window. Engraved under the crest was the word "Vanteris." He put the ring back and cut his nails on the patio. He spent the next hours on the beach, in and out of the water as fancy took him. It was after four when he returned to the villa. The telephone started to ring as he crossed the patio.

It was Szechenyi, speaking from the airport. "There's a message here from Ilona. She wants me to take a cab to the villa."

"So what's the problem?" asked Raven.

Szechenyi's voice was anxious. "It's not like her, John. If Ilona says that she'll do something, she does it."

Raven hid his impatience. The wear and tear on the other man's nervous system was beginning to tell.

"She changed her mind," he suggested. "They do it all the time. The only thing I can tell you is that she left here about ten o'clock saying that she was going to collect you."

Szechenyi was still uneasy. "She hasn't even been into her office. I just called her partner. Ilona telephoned earlier, something to do with an appointment."

"Then that's what it is," answered Raven. "Or maybe she's broken down. That car's a real menace. Take the cab as she says."

Curiosity took him into Szechenyi's bedroom. The gun was still in the clothes-closet, the five chambers loaded. He replaced the weapon and donned jeans and a shirt. He was on the patio reading when a green-and-black taxi drove through the trees. Szechenyi paid off the driver and sat down beside Raven. His face was an unhealthy colour and sweating, his seersucker suit stained and wrinkled.

"The car was seen in Madrid," he mumbled.

The news jolted Raven upright. "What do you mean, 'seen'? Who saw it?"

Szechenyi had clearly been drinking. His enunciation was unclear. "A highway patrolman on his way to work. He saw the Volkswagen parked near the Metro station."

Raven groped for his cigarettes, recreating the scene in his mind, the long stretch of boulevard, empty of traffic.

"There *was* no highway patrolman," he said with conviction. "I'd have noticed."

Szechenyi folded his lips nervously. "The car was empty. It was seven o'clock in the morning and the car was Portuguese. The man took the numbers."

The flame flared in Raven's cupped hand. "How do you know all this?"

"Alatren." Szechenyi had brought his voice under control. "He gave me a lift to the airport. He said that he has this drawer where he keeps his closed files."

Raven pointed a finger. "You're not making a lot of sense. What drawer, what files?"

Szechenyi's gesture was hopeless. "He said that a rich man like me should not have this kind of embarrassment.

He knows about the money. He knows about everything. He must have read the papers in my bag."

"How much does he want?" asked Raven.

"He didn't say. He just told me to think about things. He said that the Spanish police are . . . that they work with the Portuguese."

Raven looked beyond him at the beach. "If you make it worth his while, he'll bury the report," said Raven. "He'll know that you're lying once he checks with the frontier posts. There's bound to be a record at Beja."

Szechenyi slumped even lower, a man who has already conceded defeat. "They've still got that girl in custody," he said. "They can't find the man she was supposed to have spent the night with. It isn't so much what Alatren says as the way he says it."

Raven drew on experience. "Don't worry about him, at least for the moment. That report's worth a lot of money to him, and he's not going to jeopardize his chances. Gotsek's our problem. Do you have a number where you can reach him?"

Szechenyi shook his head. "He said that he'd be in touch."

"He'll do that all right," Raven said grimly. "Have you made up your mind what your answer will be?"

Szechenyi glanced away. He made no reply.

Raven looked at him with sudden resentment. "You haven't got long, remember. Think about what I told you in Rincón. You're on your own after tomorrow."

The telephone rang in the house, cutting short any answer that Szechenyi might have made. The two men hurried inside. Szechenyi took the call, sitting on the side of his daughter's bed. Raven watched from the doorway as the other man's face drained of colour. He said a few words in Hungarian and replaced the instrument, looking like a man who has seen his own ghost.

"Oh, my God!" he said.

"What's happening?" Raven demanded.

Szechenyi's mouth worked soundlessly, his whole body shaking. Raven ran through to the sitting-room and grabbed the brandy bottle. He held the glass as Szechenyi drank. Then he grabbed the Hungarian's chin and forced up his head.

"What happened?"

Szechenyi's scraggy neck quivered like a chicken's. Raven changed his grip to the shoulders.

"Take a hold on yourself! Who was that on the phone?"

Szechenyi struggled out an answer. "They've taken Ilona. She's been abducted!" He wiped the spittle from the corner of his mouth, looking up like a dog that is dying. "They're calling back in five minutes. If they don't get what they want, they say that they'll kill her."

Raven released him, unwilling to believe what he heard. "Who did you talk to? Was it Gotsek?"

"Ilona," Szechenyi's eyes filled with tears. "I want my girl back, John. They can have everything. I just want her back. She was crying . . ." he broke off unable to continue.

Raven saw the darkened room, the terrified woman with a gun at her head. "These are the people you wanted to trust," he said savagely. "When the call comes, I take it!"

He sat on the bed beside Szechenyi, smelling the sourness of the other man's fear. The phone rang and he lifted the handset.

Ilona's voice was unsteady. "John?"

"Let me talk to whoever is with you," he said.

"Oh, God, I'm so helpless," she said.

Somebody muffled the line at the other end. He could just hear Ilona speaking in Hungarian. Then she was back again.

"They don't want to speak to you, only my father."

"Your father's in no shape to talk to anyone," said Raven. "Tell them that. He's willing to do whatever they say. Everything's going to be all right, Ilona, I promise."

The unseen hand covered the phone again. Her voice was beginning to falter.

"They say they want the bank-transfer signed and the number of the account. They'll do the rest."

Raven relayed the news to Szechenyi who nodded dumbly. "Whatever they want," Raven said quickly.

"No police," she warned. "They say you'll be watched every inch of the way. I'm scared, John. *Please!*"

"It's all right," he soothed. "Tell them we're playing their rules. All we have to know is what they want us to do."

She spoke in a grateful rush. "Can you remember the night we went to Estoril? The three of us. You, Kirstie and me?"

"I remember." They had driven back in the moonlight, the Volkswagen open, singing the songs they had heard in the Casino.

"Take the same road from the villa. When you come to the Estoril highway turn left, as though you were going back to Lisbon. You'll see a sign at Monsanto Park that says Vale de Yeguas."

He grabbed an eyebrow pencil from the bedside table and wrote on the back of the telephone book.

"Got it! Monsanto Park Vale de Yeguas."

"Take the road to Vale de Yeguas and drive until you come to a picnic site on the edge of the forest. Take another left and you'll see a house by itself a couple of hundred yards down the track. Vila Consuela. The back door will be open. Leave the papers on the table in the sitting-room. You'll see a note telling you what to do next."

"One problem," he said quickly, motioning Szechenyi to silence. "How am I supposed to get there? I don't have transport."

She gave him a telephone number. "It's a car-hire firm in Sintra. They're expecting someone to call. The car has been booked in the name of Bates. They'll send someone out with the car. You drive him back."

Her voice wavered. He gave her the courage she clearly needed. "Don't worry. We're going to get you out of there just as soon as we can. I'm on my way now!"

He put the phone down and glanced at his watch. It was a quarter past six. He dialled the number Ilona had given him. A woman's voice answered.

"Auto Sintra!"

"Do you speak any English?"

"I do, yes, sir."

"A car was booked in the name of Bates. To go to the Vila Verde."

"One moment, please." Papers rustled. "I have the booking in front of me, sir. We have reserved for you a Ford Escort motorcar. Do you have a valid driving-licence?"

"Yes," he said impatiently. They were wasting time. "Get out here as soon as possible. Do you know the house?"

"The driver will find it," she assured him.

He hung up and turned to Szechenyi. "Have you got the bank-transfer?"

Szechenyi took the envelope from his inside pocket. The printed form was issued by the Banque Suisse et Ottomane. Raven looked at it doubtfully.

"They want your signature and the account number. Is that going to be enough?"

Szechenyi affixed his name to the transfer and printed a number. The colour was returning to his face, but his hands were still trembling. His eyes sought the dressing-table.

"The ring," he said. "The bank won't act unless the transfer is sealed with the ring."

He reached for the brandy bottle, but Raven caught his wrist. "You can drink yourself blind once this is over. How many people know about this ring?"

Szechenyi's tie was askew, giving him a slightly manic appearance. "I am not sure."

"Jesus!" said Raven. "Can't you be sure about anything? *Think!*"

Szechenyi plucked at the bedspread. "The bank took the impression of the ring when the account was first opened. I've used it ever since then. When the gold was converted to dollars. The last time was a month ago in Madrid when the man from the bank came to Madrid. He needed a signature."

Raven came to his feet. "You realize what this means? Gotsek doesn't know about the ring or else he'd have asked for it."

Szechenyi was still plucking nervously. "We have to give it to him. Not that it will make any difference. They won't let her go until the money is in their possession."

Raven slipped the signet-ring into his pocket. "Gotsek doesn't give a shit about Stephen Szechenyi. He knows you better than you know yourself. He's realized that the only way to get sense out of you is to bring you to your knees. That's exactly what he has done. The one thing he's sure about is that you don't have the guts to lie to him now. If we give him the ring, it will be as an act of good faith. He'll let her go. He knows he can pick up Ilona at any time that he wants. He's already proved it."

Szechnyi took a deep breath. "I just pray that you're right."

"I'm right," Raven said shortly. "I'm beginning to take a dislike to your friend Gotsek. He's too bloody sure of himself. What colour wax do you use for the seal?"

Szechenyi looked at him apprehensively. "It has always been red."

"It could be important," said Raven.

A car horn sounded outside. Raven ran to the window. A white Escort had drawn up beside the patio. Raven signalled the driver to wait and went through his pockets. The jeans he had on were the ones he had worn to Spain. His passport, money and driving-licence were still there.

He swung round on Szechenyi. "Call the police if you haven't heard from me by midnight. Do you understand what I'm saying? No news by midnight, *you call the police!*"

"Take my gun," urged Szechenyi, a vein worming in his forehead.

"You're out of your mind," answered Raven. "Everything's going to be all right as long as we keep our heads down. Stay close to the phone and keep off the bottle!"

He hurried outside to the car. The mechanic had moved to the passenger seat. Raven turned the ignition key. The gas tank was full. They drove six miles and he filled in the forms. Fifteen minutes later he was travelling east towards the Lisbon–Estoril highway. Gorse and rose laurel tinted the monotonous green of the park. He swung left at the exit marked Vale de Yeguas. A narrow road climbed between tall spreading cedars.

A shingle nailed to a tree pointed the way: "Vila Consuela 150 Metros." The track descended sharply, emerging out of the cedars in front of a newly constructed bungalow with a red roof and white walls. A bermuda-grass fairway beyond the house sloped away to a cluster of sand-traps. Raven switched off the engine. A two-car garage was wide open. The shutters at the front of the house were pinned back. He jumped a low wall, crossing the withered grass to the kitchen door. It was open as promised. The interior stank of stale fly-spray, and the floor and the sink were littered with dead bugs. He moved forward cautiously into the sitting-room. Nylon net curtains hung at the windows. The furniture was functional. He read the typewritten note on the table.

Go to the Café Bahia, 84 Rossio. Wait there for a telephone call.

He stuffed the note in his back pocket and lifted the phone on impulse. The ringing tone told him it was functioning. He froze as something whirred in the kitchen, relaxing when he recognized the sound of the refrigerator motor. He opened the door opposite with a feeling that someone was watching him. A double bed faced the window. The scarf that Ilona had been wearing was draped from the head of the bed. Strips of adhesive tape lay on the floor, twisted and stuck as though used and discarded. He retreated slowly to the sitting-room. There were hundreds of villas like this, he thought, built for golfers. It was a perfect location to hold a hostage.

Raven placed Szechenyi's envelope on the table and left the house as he had entered. The feeling persisted that someone was watching him. A flurry of paper on the breeze drew his attention to the garage. There was nothing inside but a fragment of broken tail-light glittering on the concrete floor.

Rossio was an eighteenth-century square with heroic statues and mosaic pavements. This was the real heart of Lisbon, noisy, vulgar and dirty. Raven parked the Ford on the north side of the square where the buildings jostled one another like city commuters. The Café Bahia occupied the two bottom floors of a yellowing edifice. Raven walked through the entrance. The long bar was deserted. He ordered a coffee and waited for what came next. The barman picked up the phone, plugging one ear with a finger as he looked in Raven's direction. He slid the handset along the bar. Raven lifted the receiver.

Ilona's voice was jubilant. "I'm free, John, free! I still can't believe it!"

He bent into the mouthpiece. "Where are you speaking from?"

"Outside the zoo. Do you know how to get there?"

"I'll find it," he said.

"I'm in a phone booth in front of the main entrance. I'll wait until you get here. Hurry!"

"I'm on my way," he replied.

He threw some coins on the counter and hurried outside. The approach to the zoo merged into an open space criss-crossed by streetcar tracks. It was closing time, and the keepers were herding the visitors towards the exits. The crowds surged through the gates, swamping the transport waiting outside. Raven leaned out through the open window. Ilona was standing close to the zoo railings. He touched the horn a couple of times, drawing her attention. She ran towards him, her hair flying, and collapsed in the seat beside him.

She drew her arm away, wincing as he touched it. The skin on her wrists was chafed and angry. Her ankles displayed the same marks. Her eyes followed his as he glanced across the streetcar tracks.

"They'd already gone when I called you," she said quietly, taking the cigarette he offered.

He gave her a light. "Where's your car?"

"Campo Grande. Outside the Metro station." Her face was tight, but she seemed to have gone through the worst of it.

"Have you called your father yet?"

She nodded. "Was he drinking when you left?"

"I'd say he was thinking seriously about it," he smiled. "This is one time he can't be blamed. He's had about as much as he can take, one way and another. What the hell happened, Ilona?"

She blew smoke nervously. "In the first place, I never even got as far as Lisbon. There was this policeman standing in the middle of the road just outside Mem Martins, flagging me down. My first thought was that there had been an accident. Then he asked for my papers. As soon as I opened the door, he was in the car, holding this pistol on me. We drove like that to Campo Grande. There was another man there, waiting with a car. They forced me inside. I was terrified; I was sure they were going to kill me. Once we had reached the villa, they tied me up and put a blindfold on me. All I could do was just lie there. It was horrible."

He gave her the scarf. "I brought this back with me. When did Gotsek show up?"

The zoo gates were closing on the last of the stragglers.

"Later. I could hear but I couldn't see. They'd already made me call the office and the airport. Then Gotsek arrived. He was the one who made me call Papa."

She blinked hard, struggling to hold back the tears. "Easy," he urged, moved by a rush of sympathy. "What exactly did Gotsek say? It's important."

She brushed her eyes with the back of her hand. "He talked about you, for one thing."

"Me?" he said, disturbed by the news.

"He knows exactly who you are. He'd got this idea that you've been encouraging Papa to hold out. He thinks that you've got some kind of interest. I mean in the money."

He gulped smoke into his lungs and exhaled. "I suppose that tipped the balance. Maybe it's just as well. It might be the best thing that could happen. Now for the bad news. The Volkswagen was seen in Madrid."

She gasped, staring wide-eyed at him. "But how? Who saw us?"

"The car, not us," he replied. "A highway patrolman on his way to work. Alatren told your father. He's sitting on the report until he makes up his mind how much it is worth. They're all very pleased with themselves, for the moment at least."

She dropped her cigarette outside. "Why do you say it like that? 'For the moment, at least'?"

"Because that's what it is," he said. "For the moment."

Her face relaxed but her eyes were still curious. "Gotsek said to get rid of you, that you're a trouble-maker."

He grinned in spite of himself. "He doesn't know how right he is. I can promise you one thing, Ilona. You can forget about Gotsek from now on."

She used the mirror on the back of the sunshield. "Can we get my car, please?"

He swung the Ford into the stream of traffic. Old men were sitting on the benches in Campo Grande, nodding in the sunshine.

"Behind the ice-cream cart," she said, pointing.

Raven could see the front end of the Volkswagen, parked across the road, facing them.

He reached across and unfastened the door for her. "Go on home and wait there for me. Don't move until I get back."

She leaned through the lowered window. "Where are you going?"

"Just go on home and wait for me," he repeated.

He watched until she had the Volkswagen moving. There was no one following her. He drove down town to the main post office. A line was waiting to use the overseas telephone booths. When his turn finally came, he found his lawyer still in his office, a tape of *The Ring* playing in the background.

"It's me," Raven said quickly. "I need your help."

O'Callaghan's voice was long-suffering. "What else? I thought you were supposed to be in Portugal."

"I am," said Raven. "That Canadian I met at your birthday party, the one who lives in Lisbon. Cameron Duncan. How well do you know him?"

"What kind of question is that? I know him well, why?"

"Is he the sort of guy I can talk to?"

"Of course you can talk to him," O'Callaghan replied. "Look, will you make it quick? What do you want to talk to Duncan about?"

"I'm not sure. Isn't he married to a judge's daughter?"

"The judge died six months ago. What the hell's going on, John?"

Raven laid a piece of paper on top of the coin-box. "Where does he live?" He waited as the lawyer searched his address book.

"Praca Latino Coelho 4. The telephone number is 555-849."

Raven wrote it down. "I want you to call him just as soon as I put the phone down, Patrick. Say that I may be getting in touch."

Caution leaked into his friend's voice. "Is that all that you're going to tell me?"

"That's all there is to tell at the moment," said Raven. "And not a word of this to Kirstie, OK?"

The lawyer lowered the volume on his tape-machine. "We saw her last night as a matter of fact. She had some people in for drinks—Maggie Sanchez and the film crew. I didn't get the chance to talk to her much, but Maureen says that she was in an odd mood. There's nothing wrong between you two, is there?"

"Not a thing that can't be handled," said Raven. "Just one last piece of information. The man Saxon, is he still at the home office?"

O'Callaghan's tone sharpened. "This isn't another rescue operation, is it? One of your political friends in need of asylum?"

"Just answer the question," Raven said patiently.

"Saxon's still at the home office, yes. But if this is what I think it is, you can approach him yourself this time."

"I'll do that," said Raven. "I should be in London some time tomorrow."

O'Callaghan was plainly surprised. "But Kirstie's supposed to be flying back to Lisbon on Monday."

"Not any more," said Raven. "She doesn't know it yet and I don't want her to. Let me break the news myself when the time comes. Don't even say that I called you."

"Tomorrow is Sunday," O'Callaghan reminded him.

"I know what day it is," Raven replied and put the phone down.

It was after eight o'clock when he drove through the umbrella pines. The last of the sun gilded the stony headlands. The lavender shadows had lost their sharpness. He wheeled the Ford in beside the Volkswagen and touched the horn-button. Ilona called as he went up the steps from the patio.

"In the kitchen!"

They were sitting at the table, Ilona on one side, her father facing her. The brandy bottle and Szechenyi's glass were at his elbow. Ilona had changed into slacks and a man's shirt. The long sleeves hid her lacerated wrists.

Her eyes sought Raven warningly. "Did anyone call?" he asked, pulling up a chair.

She shook her head. "Papa wants to say something."

Szechenyi spoke with drunken dignity.

"I just wanted to say that we owe you more than we can repay, John. You are a true friend."

The dripping tap accentuated the silence that followed. Raven extended his arm, laying his closed fist knuckles down on the table. He opened his fingers slowly, revealing the signet-ring concealed in his palm.

Szechenyi's glass fell, rolling from the table and smashing on the floor. Ilona grabbed a cloth, looking up as Raven put the ring back in his pocket.

"We're playing my rules now," he said quietly. "Ilona's here and that's all that matters."

Szechenyi refilled the glass Ilona gave him, his hand trembling. The last few seconds appeared to have destroyed him again. His voice cracked painfully.

"Gotsek will know. He will think we have tricked him!"

Ilona crossed the room like a cat in a strange place. "Gotsek will know what?"

Raven leaned back comfortably. "The bank-transfer is meant to be sealed with your father's ring. It's useless without it."

"You will give me the ring," said Szechenyi, extending his hand.

"All in good time," said Raven. "You're going to England, the pair of you."

Ilona's eyes burned like lasers. "You gambled with my life! Is that what you're saying?"

Raven was still watching Ilona. Brief though the affair had been with her, the memory of it was exciting.

"Relax," he said. "There *was* never a gamble! If Gotsek had asked for the ring, I'd have given it to him. He just didn't know what he needed, and by the time that he does, it'll be too late."

Szechenyi's liver-spotted hands were still shaking. "How can you say that? They have someone in the bank in their pay. We already know that!"

"No," said Raven. "There is no danger. Today's Saturday. Swiss banks open at eight o'clock on Monday. There's no possible way that Gotsek could know before then. By then we'll be in England, all three of us."

Ilona's face was stony. "And what do we do in England?"

"In the first place, you get the protection you need. You people have to forget about Spain and Portugal. Just walk away from everything. Businesses, homes, personal possessions, the lot! We'll leave in the morning. You can stay with Kirstie and me on the boat until we find somewhere more permanent. There are people there in a position to help, people in high places."

Szechenyi rose unsteadily. He staggered towards the bedrooms, clutching the brandy bottle. His daughter's voice filled with bitter accusation.

"Have you any idea what you've just done to us?"

"I've saved your life, for one thing," he answered. A sense of outrage sent his blood rising. "And I've made you rich, which is all that you really care about. You don't care about your father, Ilona. The only person you're concerned with is yourself."

Her face flared as though he had struck her. "Do you really hate me that much?"

"I don't hate anyone," he answered steadily. "In a way, I'm sorry for you."

She smiled, her husky voice defiant. "The one thing I don't need is pity, especially yours."

He knew in that second that she was right, that *she* was the one who needed nobody. She had taken her own failing and foisted it onto him. The phone bell rang, startling them.

"I'll get it," he said.

"I love you," she answered.

He picked up the receiver. "Hello?"

"This is Cameron Duncan. I'd like to speak to John Raven."

"Speaking," said Raven. The flat prairie drawl evoked the memory of a large man with black gypsy eyes, a laugh that started deep in his belly, and hair the colour of fresh steel filings.

"I just had a call from Patrick O'Callaghan. He gave me your number. What can I do for you?"

Raven lowered his voice. "I'm not sure yet, but I may need your help, a sort of man-on-the-spot manoeuvre. Look, I can't talk now. Is there any chance of seeing you later this evening?"

"Sure," said Duncan. "We're in tonight. Drop over any time. Do you know where we are?"

"Praca Latino Coelho, right?"

"Number four. I take it you have wheels?"

"Right," said Raven. "Things are a little uncertain this end. I can't give you a definite time. Do you want me to call you again before I leave?"

"Hell, no," said Duncan. "Just come!"

Szechenyi's room was open. He was lying on the bed with the bottle clutched to his stomach. Raven made his way out to the patio. Cicadas chorused harshly in the fading daylight. Ilona was sitting on the swing. The bitterness had gone from her voice.

"Did you hear what I said just now?" she asked huskily.

"I heard."

"And that's all that you have to say?" She spoke like a woman with no more defences left.

"Look," he said impulsively. "I've got a weird feeling that somehow I'm being had. I can't put my finger on it but the feeling is there. I'm going to make sure we get out tomorrow without any hassle. I'm going into Lisbon."

"You do what you have to do," she answered quietly. "We seem to be in your hands."

He pulled out his car keys, relieved that the tension between them had ended. "Keep an eye on your father. The best place for him is bed."

"You will be back?"

"I'll be back," he said. He gave her Duncan's telephone number. "Don't call unless it's an emergency."

She took the slip of paper, her face close in the half-light. "It isn't too late for us, John." Her voice was almost a whisper. She was in the house by the time he had the Ford going.

He bought a flashlight in a filling station on his way to the golf-course. The rented car bumped down through the cedars. Instinct had drawn him back to the Vila Consuela. Gotsek was a chess player moves ahead of his opponents. Much of what Raven had said earlier had been wishful thinking. He had never really imagined that Ilona would be released so easily, and he still feared a trap. With any kind of luck, the villa might provide a clue.

Someone had locked the back door since his last visit. He used an elbow to break a pane of glass and climbed into the kitchen sink. The envelope had gone from the sitting-room table, the strips of adhesive tape removed from the bedroom floor. He turned his head slowly, an elusive memory floating just out of reach. He sat on the edge of the table. His brain cleared suddenly, illuminated by a flash of total recall. He ran through the kitchen, slipped the catch on the door, and aimed his light into the garage. The beam found the glass on the concrete floor. He bent down, shining the flash on the fragment of broken tail-light. The maker's name and model number were moulded into the glass. He put the fragment in his pocket and walked back into the house.

He dialled Vila Verde and Ilona answered. "Thank God," she burst out. "I need you here. My father's out on the patio. He's gone beyond me, John. I can't do a thing with him."

"I'll be back as soon as I can," he answered. "Can you remember what sort of car they used to drive you to the Vila Consuela?"

"A Mercedes," she said. "Why do you ask?"

"I had an idea I was being followed," he told her. "But it's the wrong make of car. Try to get your father in the house. Do whatever he wants as long as you get him into bed."

He replaced the phone and dialled England. Kirstie's voice came loud and clear.

"Don't waste time!" he instructed. "Just listen to me! Do *not* leave London until you hear from me. And don't call the villa. Is that clear?"

She clawed her way down a thousand miles of cable, refusing to let him go. "You can't do this to me, I'm your wife! What the hell's going on?"

"I'm not too sure," he said truthfully. "But I'm beginning to have some doubts. You'd better prepare yourself for a shock."

He broke the connection. The air outside was cool and fresh after the staleness of the villa. The key of the puzzle had slotted into place; the trick now was to assemble the other pieces. He drove past cedars looming like sentries in the glare of the headlamps. Traffic coming from the city locked him in for the next eight miles. The last part of the journey took him into the wooded hills behind Sintra, past a prison with machine-gun emplacements stark in the moonlight. He started the long ascent to Sintra, setting the wipers in motion as fog clung to the windshield. It was almost nine o'clock when he turned onto the track through the pines. He killed the motor, ghosting the last fifty yards with his lights off. The French windows were closed, the light above illuminating the empty patio.

He slipped out of the car, wings whirring in the darkness behind him. He waited until the bird had resettled, then crept towards the carport. He aimed the flash at the rear of the Volkswagen. The piece of broken glass in his hand matched the damaged tail-lamp.

He straightened his back. What he had guessed was now confirmed. He walked across the patio to the darkened sitting-room. The rest of the house was in darkness. He rattled the door-handle and called Ilona's name. The lights came on. Ilona came forward and unlocked the French windows. He was inside before he saw that she was holding her father's gun in her hand, her face expressionless. There was no sign of Szechenyi.

"What's happening?" he said, looking towards the darkened kitchen.

She moved her shoulder, long hair swinging. "See for yourself!"

He followed her along the corridor to her bedroom. She stood in the doorway pointing. Szechenyi was lying face down across the bed. His fall had taken the telephone-table with him. The instrument was in a pool of vomit. Raven straightened the table and opened both windows.

"How the hell did he get in this state?"

Her shoulders lifted. "He finished the bottle and wanted more. I tried to stop him but he broke the cupboard open."

He took the gun from her hand. "And this?"

She turned a long level glance on him. "He was going to kill himself."

Szechenyi tried to raise his head, but the effort was too much. Raven pulled him up onto the bed.

"Let's go," said Raven, stuffing the gun into his belt. "You and I have some talking to do."

They faced one another across the kitchen-table. Ilona spoke first. "You realize that this is our last chance. I mean that literally."

"Our last chance for what?"

Her voice was controlled, almost conversational. "To sort out our lives. We need one another."

"You're crazy," he said.

She gave him look for look. "If we don't take this chance, we'll regret it for the rest of our lives."

Even now he wanted to spare her. "Listen to me, Ilona. You're a very sick woman. You're in need of help. Tell me the truth and I'll do what I can for you."

She gave him a far-away smile, her eyes like oiled slate. "The truth?"

"I've just come from the villa," he said steadily. "I found this on the floor of the garage." He put the broken piece of tail-lamp on the table.

Her face was that of a child detected in some trivial fault.

"You can forget the acting," he said. "It's over, Ilona. You weren't abducted. You drove out there yourself. You staged the whole business. I want to know why. Why did you lie to your father, to me?"

She rose and drew a glass of water at the sink. "Ask my father why," she said, challenging him across the room. "My life has been full of lies."

"I'm asking you," he said. "And you're going to have to tell me. Time's running out."

"I wanted you for myself," she said, coming forward. "I wanted to share things with you."

The outrageousness of her statement, her composure, reinforced his belief that her mind was unhinged.

"It's over," he said, still trying to reason with her. "You've got to understand, Ilona. You've got to face the truth about yourself."

She smiled as if at some unpleasant memory. "Papa thinks that you're after the money. You still have the signet-ring."

He pushed the ring across the table, repelled by the accusation. "Do you know what I'm going to do, Ilona? I'm going to pack my things and walk right out of this place. From now on, you people can play your games with somebody else. I never want to set eyes on you again for the rest of my life."

She made no move to pick up the ring, staring at him as though fixing his face in her mind. Szechenyi had come to himself, muttering as Raven walked past the doorway. Raven scooped the clothes from the hanging rail and emptied the drawers in the dressing-table. He carried the two bags along the corridor. She was still sitting at the kitchen-table. He put the gun on the sitting-room tallboy.

"You're on your own," he said shortly. "Don't count on me any more!"

He threw the bags in the back of the Ford and stood for a moment, sucking the salt-laden air into his lungs. There were four hours to go before the airport shut down for the night. What he wanted was the first plane out with a vacant seat. He was about to take the wheel when a shot rang out. The echo sang through the trees, losing itself in the caves below. He swung round, facing the house. The lights were still on. It was as if the report only existed in his mind. Then he heard her talking in Portuguese. He tiptoed across the flower-beds and flattened himself against the wall, inching sideways until he could see into her bedroom.

She was standing by the bed, holding the telephone in rubber-gloved hands. The acrid stink of burnt cordite drifted through the open windows. Szechenyi was face down on the floor, his arms and legs splayed. Blood welled from a black hole in the back of his head, staining his hair and neck crimson. His daughter used her voice like a cello, gesticulating with her free hand as she spoke. Most of what she said made no sense to him, but a few key words sank into his brain. He heard his own name, carefully spelled, the Portuguese words for "dead" and "father."

He backed off slowly, keeping her in sight, then ran for the car, his bronchial tubes wheezing. The motor fired at the first attempt, and the car shot forward behind the full glare of the headlamps. He swung left at the crossroads, taking a minor road that coiled like a snake around the mountain. He kept his foot down on the accelerator, scarring the road surface with brake burns as he took the bends. He drove with one eye on the rear-view mirror, cold sweat dripping down his flanks. The floodlit battlements of Sintra Castle loomed above. The route he had chosen turned in a series of loops, avoiding the centre of the city. The narrow road had been blasted out of solid rock. Railings unwound in the headlamps. Beyond them was a six-hundred-foot drop to the restless ocean. He drove for eleven miles without meeting another vehicle. A left turn took him towards the distant lights of Estoril. A gas station lifted out of the darkness, yellow and green under dusty eucalyptus-trees. A pay phone sign hung outside the lighted office. Raven pulled in behind the pumps and a youth emerged yawning.

"Telephone," said Raven, pointing inside.

Cameron Duncan's voice came on the line. "I have to see you," said Raven. The attendant was studying the Ford. "I've reason to think that I could be in trouble."

"You are!" said Duncan. "Where the hell are you speaking from?"

A mound of empty crates hid the road sign across the road. Raven opened the office door, getting a better view.

"I'm in a Sacavem station, about eight miles out of Sintra on the way to Estoril."

"Let me get a map!" There was a rustle of paper. "OK, I've got it. Can you get that car you're driving out of sight?"

The youth had moved from the Ford and was watching the road, reflectively picking his nose.

"I'm not too sure," said Raven. "There's some kind of workshop, but the only person here is the pump-attendant."

"Right," said Duncan. "Now listen. The police are looking for you. They've got your name, description and the number of the car you're driving. It was on the air just twenty minutes ago."

Raven licked his lips, tasting blood or salt, he no longer knew which. "Is that all they say?"

"I'm afraid there's more. Anyone who gets sight of you is meant to call this number they gave. You're wanted for murder."

In a weird way the news eased Raven's mind. At least he knew how he stood.

"It's a setup," he said. "I didn't kill anyone."

"Let me talk to this guy," said Duncan.

Raven opened the office door again and beckoned the youth across. The attendant listened to Duncan's fluent Portuguese and handed the phone back to Raven. "I've told him your car's on the blink," said Duncan. "He's going to let you put it in the workshop. The mechanics will look at it on Monday morning. It can stay buried there for a month if we're lucky. Do you have any luggage with you?"

"A couple of bags," said Raven.

"Get them out of the car. Leave nothing in it that belongs to you. Stand near the road where the guy can't see who picks you up. I'll be there just as soon as I can."

The youth unlocked a sliding door to the workshop. Fluorescent lighting in the iron girders illuminated motionless machinery. Raven took out his bags and the flashlight and drove the Ford forward. The attendant closed the doors again.

"*Inglês?*" he asked curiously, pointing a dirty finger at Raven.

Raven shook his head. It had taken him forty minutes to drive eighteen miles, travelling a circle for most of the way.

The police had been prompt to get their message on the air. The attendant was plainly prepared to continue the discussion in sign language if necessary. Raven carried his bags to the roadside. The attendant was back in his office, transistor blaring.

Raven tapped a cigarette from the pack, running the picture of his flight in his mind. He froze the frame with Ilona talking into the phone, her husky voice agitated, her face wearing the mask of insanity. He remembered the rubber gloves she'd been wearing. He had handled the gun three or four times. His prints were bound to be on it. Every move she had made was guided by cunning. Madness created its own reality. He moved from one side of the road to the other, keeping out of sight as the occasional car flashed by. Half an hour went by with no sign of Duncan. Raven squatted on his bags, his eyes on the road. He heard the whine of the motor long before he saw the vehicle. The driver was using his gears on the bends. There was a final burst of speed and a battered Porsche appeared. Salt and sun had destroyed the bloom of the paintwork. Rust scarred the dents in the fenders. A press card bearing a maple-leaf was fixed on the inside of the windshield.

The driver eased himself from the wheel. A couple of inches shorter than Raven, he had the build of a hockey defenceman. His bright silver hair was cropped short, his skin deeply tanned. He was wearing a blue shirt with short sleeves and a pair of stained cords.

He grabbed Raven's bags and threw them into the Porsche. "Let's get out of here quickly. I don't want this guy to see the car."

Raven stretched out gratefully, the top of his head almost touching the roof. Duncan let in the clutch and the Porsche leaped forward. The bodywork was shabby but the motor was finely tuned. The Canadian drove fast and with confidence, zigzagging cross-country until he found the spot he was looking for. He swung the car off the road, tyres clawing the verge, and into a jungle of oleanders. He stopped the motor and pulled a flat tin box from his pocket. He rolled a fat joint from the grass inside, lit it and passed it across. Raven shook his head. The seeds crackled as Duncan inhaled. The inside of the car filled with the smell of a bonfire.

"You are in one big heap of trouble," said the Canadian. The announcement was a statement of fact, not a criticism.

Raven nodded. "I know it. And even that could be an understatement." He lowered his window, letting the pungent fumes drift out into the darkness.

The glow from the joint lit Duncan's face. "These people want you for murder, my friend."

"I know what they want me for," Raven replied. "The point is I'm innocent."

"I called Patrick before I left the house. I told him what happened. He's getting in touch with your wife."

"Jesus Christ!" said Raven, driving the heel of his hand at his forehead.

"He flipped," said Duncan and coughed. "God*dam!* this stuff is fierce! Patrick told me to lock you up somewhere safe and get hold of a good lawyer. He's flying out tomorrow with your wife."

"Lock me up somewhere safe," Raven repeated incredulously.

"Keep you under wraps until the moment is right," said Duncan. "It's my idea."

Raven reached for the joint. He sucked down the stinging smoke, retaining it in his lungs for as long as he could.

"And when the moment's right?"

"Look," the Canadian's voice was understanding. "You want to tell me as much or as little as you please, I don't give a goddam. But I have to know something if I'm going to help."

He turned out to be a good listener, interrupting only when Raven's narrative flagged. Raven kept nothing back.

When the story was told, Duncan switched on the multiband radio. He moved the pointer across the lighted dial, picking up call-signs and fragments of conversation. He turned the set off.

"It looks as though they've forgotten you, at least for the moment."

"They haven't forgotten me," Raven said. "That's one thing you can safely bet on."

"Let me ask you something," said Duncan. "Do you know the name of this clinic Ilona Szechenyi was in?"

"I think it was called the Clínica Galvez."

"That was the name," said Duncan. "I know it well."

They stared at one another in the glow from the end of the smoke. "I'd like to get one thing straight," Duncan said suddenly. "I'm here for two reasons. In the first place, I owe Patrick. In the second place, I'm a pro. If a story's a good one, I'll run my nose up its ass to get it. But I do have scruples. For a journalist, that is. There'll be no story filed by me until you're safely off the hook. But once you *are* off the hook then the story is mine. Do we have a deal or not?"

Raven took the Canadian's hand. "We've got a deal."

"Good," said Duncan briskly. "Let me tell you something about Portuguese justice. You get a fair enough trial. The trick is getting yourself into a court-room. They can keep you hanging around for a year or more before they bring you in front of a jury."

"I'm obliged for the information," Raven said, squinting. "But I hadn't planned on going to jail."

"A courageous statement for a guy in your position. Tell me about the brother. You think she killed him too?"

"I'm pretty sure of it now," answered Raven. "It's easy enough to see, looking back. She knew what she was going to do before we took off for Spain. She left me there, sitting in the car, walked in and stuck an ice-pick in her brother's chest. Then she jammed the lock on the front door, came out and fetched me. I've no doubt at all that it went like that."

"I'll buy that," said Duncan, looking at his watch. "You were the perfect patsy. Not only that, you gave her story credibility. What puzzles me is the motivation. Why did she have to kill her brother?"

"That's easy," said Raven. "To start with, he was an asshole. She couldn't afford to let him get anywhere near that money. He would have had the lot, and her name was already on it. No half a million for her."

Duncan held up a placatory hand. "I'm only being the devil's advocate. OK, so she gets rid of the brother and throws in her lot with the father. But he's seen the light. I mean, he's ready to trade, which is not what the lady wants. She drives back to Portugal, brain working at the speed of light, and goes into the abduction caper. I have to admit, I'm getting a sneaking admiration for this chick. She's resourceful, to say the least."

"It's a pity the pair of you don't meet," Raven said drily.

Duncan eased a hole in his belt and belched. "Now for the sixty-four-dollar question. Why doesn't she just sit tight and wait for her father to die? That way, she inherits the whole shooting match."

"Because her father was still alive is why. She wants everything *now*. So she shoots him and frames me. It's called killing two birds with one stone."

Duncan brought his hands together in one sharp report. "The problem's to prove all this. It's a pity that my wife's father isn't still with us. He had a real sneaky mind."

A blaze of headlamps illuminated the surrounding darkness. Raven ducked low as a car passed heading for Sintra.

"You've said nothing about Gotsek," he said, struggling up again. "Or don't you believe in people like that?"

Duncan made a sound of derision. "I can show you a Gotsek right here in Lisbon. Second secretary to the Bulgarian embassy, the guy who master-minded the killing in London. The one where they shot two hundred cc of deadly poison into a man called Markov. With a bloody umbrella, no less. Yes, I believe in Gotsek."

"Thank God for that," said Raven. "There are times when I find myself wondering whether the whole thing isn't some kind of ghastly nightmare."

Duncan thought for a moment. "We're going to have to gamble," he decided. "Gamble on which way a particular cop's mind works."

"I *know* the way their minds work," answered Raven. "I used to be one myself. Basically they're all the same. Once they've got a suspect, they're not looking to prove him innocent. They want a conviction. Stephen Szechenyi is dead and his daughter claims that I'm responsible. My fingerprints are all over the murder weapon, and they'll find a motive."

"So what do you want to do—run?" Duncan crossed his legs.

"I'm running now," answered Raven. "And I don't like it one little bit. Make me a better proposition."

The Canadian nodded. "I was just about to do that very thing. The Toronto *Inquirer* may not mean much to you, but it does have clout. If we can get the proof we need, I can guarantee the backup. What did you do with this glass you found in the garage?"

"I left it at the Vila Verde. On the kitchen-table."

"That didn't help any," Duncan answered. "She'll claim that her tail-lamp's been broken for months. What we need is something concrete, proof of what we're saying. Let's go out to this place where she claims she was held. There just might be something you missed."

"I doubt it," said Raven. "The lady cleans house well except for the things she wants to be found."

Duncan turned the ignition key, speaking over the clatter of the engine. "I've said this before. There's an aura of evil charm about this woman that I find fascinating." The Porsche headlamps came on with full power, staring across the deserted vineyards. "Which way?"

"Monsanto Park," said Raven.

The Porsche bumped down through the cedars. The moon cast a spectral radiance over the fairway. Duncan stopped the car, looking across at the whitewashed villa.

"I'll get the door," Raven said quickly. He climbed through the broken window and unlocked the front door. He found the switch and the light came on. He pointed across at the bedroom.

"There were some bits of adhesive tape on the floor. They were gone when I came back the second time."

Duncan walked through the house, opening and shutting closets and drawers. He came back into the sitting-room wiping his hands.

"I don't think this place has ever been lived in. There are no sheets, nothing in the kitchen, not even cups and saucers. Is the phone working?"

"It was." Raven lifted the receiver and heard a dialling tone. "It still is."

Duncan composed a number, using the phone as if the person at the other end of the line were in front of him, smiling and gesturing.

"Angie, darling! It's Cam Duncan. I'm after some information. The Monsanto Golf Club, between the fourth and fifth holes. There's a house by itself near the cedars. That's right, just below the picnic area. Do you happen to know who owns it? You'll call me back? Fine! I'll give you the number, I'm not at home." He read the number from the plastic disc in front of him.

Then he put the phone down and winked. "Angie Farr. She's got a real-estate office in Cascais." He felt in his pocket for something to write with.

The phone rang almost immediately. He listened, scribbling on a piece of paper. "I'll talk to you soon, Angie, you're a treasure."

He put the phone down and turned to Raven. "This place belongs to some people from Mozambique. They built it for rental income. An outfit called the Agência Caparica handles the business end. Where did you say Ilona's business is located?"

"Rossio. Number eighty-three." The joint had left Raven hungry.

"Let's get out of here," Duncan said quickly. "It's the same address as the Agência Caparica."

It was after nine o'clock when they reached the city. Duncan stopped the Porsche on a quiet street near the opera-house, in front of a narrow building with a plate-glass front.

"Don't worry," said Duncan. "The place is empty until Monday morning. Bring your bags in with you."

He unlocked the entrance, letting Raven into a softly lit lobby with mosaics commemorating the discoveries of Vasco da Gama. A board on the wall bore the names of the tenants. Most of them were professional men: architects, lawyers and a couple of medical consultants. The entire penthouse floor was occupied by the Toronto *Inquirer*. The elevator opened into a reception area with dull red walls and an off-white carpet. Comfortable chairs were placed near magazine racks and reading-tables. The top of the large desk had been cleared except for a bowl of freesias and a hooded word processor.

Duncan led the way down the passage, tapping on doors as they passed. "This is the library! Jake Engel's studio, he's our photographer. This is where the girls work and this is the power-house!"

He opened the last door. A bank of graduated angle-lights came on in the ceiling. Duncan increased the brilliance, lighting every corner of the room. Raven was no stranger to the bustle of a newspaper office, and he'd been to parties in the panelled sanctuaries of Bloomsbury publishers. But this was something beyond his experience. The entire outer wall of the room was glass. Two doors offered access to a flat roof where jacaranda-trees grew in tubs surrounded by garden furniture. A plain pine table served as a desk and carried four telephones. At the side of the table was a telex machine. Silk rugs from Macao hung on the walls. The only seats were four enormous club armchairs upholstered in suede. A Perspex map of the world displayed the time in five continents. A framed certificate hung in a corner.

THE LIVERMORE AWARD
FOR
INVESTIGATIVE JOURNALISM
1981
Cameron Duncan of the Toronto *Inquirer*

A gift-shop shingle below read "Time flies when you're having fun!"

Duncan opened the French windows. The view from the terrace outside was staggering. The roofs of the old city descended like steps lit by lanterns as far as the waterfront, where ships were being unloaded in the glare from overhead gantries. Duncan opened another door. This time it was a bathroom with a full-size tub and a shower-stall. Next to this was a well-stocked bar.

"You name it," said Duncan. "We don't believe in stinting ourselves."

"Whisky and water, no ice," said Raven. "And make it a light one, please. I'm trying to remember when I ate last."

Duncan poured the drinks and rolled himself another joint. A cloud of smoke surrounded his head.

"You'll have to wait for food," he said. "We've got business to mind. If you want to put your feet up, I recommend the sofa."

The sofa was the size of a bed and matched the arm-

chairs. Raven lowered himself gratefully, the Scotch lighting a small comfortable blaze in his stomach. His legs were
beginning to ache again. He rolled up his jeans and looked
at his calf muscles.

"Varicose veins," he explained.

Duncan touched a switch, activating a motor that pulled
eight yards of lined velvet along the curtain rail. He
shrugged when Raven refused the joint.

"How much Portuguese do you speak?"

"Just a few words," Raven said from the sofa. "I've been
making out with a phrase-book."

"No matter," said Duncan. "When you've finished your
drink, we have a call to make. I'll do the talking."

The elevator deposited them back in the discreetly lit
lobby. The flight of steps across the street climbed to the
opera-house. It was the intermission, and dinner-jacketed
lovers of Mozart clustered outside the theatre, chatting and
smoking. Duncan negotiated the one-way system with fa-
miliarity, twisting right and left through a succession of
darkened streets into the blaze of Rossio. The shops were
closed, but the restaurants and bars were still busy. The Canadian manoeuvred the Porsche into an empty space on the
west side of the vast square. He killed the motor and
scraped his fingers through his short hair.

"That's it, right across the square. Preserve an air of authority and keep your mouth shut!"

They walked through the crowded sidewalk tables. A
metal plate screwed to the door of the building displayed a
disembodied eye, emblem of a security service. Duncan
winked and pressed the night-bell firmly. He was holding
his press card at the ready. A light showed in the transom,
and the door opened on a short length of chain. A disgrun-
tled-looking man wearing a pyjama jacket over his trousers
peered out through the crack. A nickel-plated whistle hung
on a string round his neck.

"*Policia!*" Duncan held up his press card.

The building superintendent unfastened the chain and pulled back the door. Duncan and Raven pushed forward into the lobby. The tile floor was worn, the colours faded. A flight of stairs descended to the basement. The superintendent shifted uncomfortably under Duncan's scrutiny. The two men spoke earnestly before going down the steps to the basement.

The Canadian came back alone. He produced a passkey as the elevator gate started its rise. "Your girl-friend borrowed this during the lunch-hour. She gave the super some bullshit story about locking herself out. She returned the key about half an hour later."

He opened the cage and found a switch, lighting the corridor as far as the fire-escape at the end. He started to read the names on a board.

"Duarte Limitada, SAFOR, dental repairs, the translation bureau, gold and silver bought for cash and—here you are—Agência Caparica!"

The passkey worked smoothly. The small office was hung with posters of Madeira and the Algarve. The neat desk had been cleared for the weekend. A can of instant coffee and a mug stood on top of a metal filing cabinet. It looked like a one-man business.

Light from a revolving sign on the roof laid a pattern through the venetian blinds.

"Stand back!" said Duncan, rubbing his hands and grinning. "I'm hot!"

He tried the locked filing cabinet. Raven leaned against the wall, watching. His mind was already made up about Duncan. The man's style was bizarre but it inspired confidence.

The journalist yanked a drawer in the desk and tipped its contents onto the floor. Each of the twenty-odd keys bore a name-tag. Duncan leaned down, balancing himself and whistling softly. He struck like a cat at a mouse, straightening up to show the key he was holding.

"Vila Consuela!" he proclaimed. "The agency closes from
one until three, and there's a locksmith on every street from
here to Alfama. Any one of them would have cut a key for
her. She puts the original back and no one's the wiser. I tell
you, man, this chick had everything worked out."

Raven came off the wall. "The girl she works with says
Ilona never came near the office today."

"What she means," said Duncan, "is that she didn't see
her."

He put the drawer back and tidied the top of the desk,
making sure that nothing was out of place. They locked up
the office and walked to the end of the corridor. A drop-bar
opened the way to the fire-escape. A flight of iron stairs zig-
zagged down to a yard lined with garbage cans. A door led
to the street.

Duncan nodded with assurance. "That's the way she
came in and left. She borrows the passkey from the super,
has a copy cut of the key to the villa and disappears again.
The only person who sees her is the super."

The man was waiting for them down in the lobby. He
took the passkey and let them out of the building. Once in
the car, Raven glanced up at the rear-view mirror.

"The door's still open. He's watching us."

"Who gives a shit?" said Duncan. "He can't see the numbers at that distance. In any case, he doesn't know it yet but
he's on his way to fame. This is all building into a nice little
story."

He switched on the radio once the car was moving, in-
terpreting the nasal Portuguese.

"A murder hunt has been mounted by Lisbon detectives,
aided by specialized units of the Guarda Republicana. The
authorities are seeking an Englishman named John Raven,
forty-two years of age, one metre ninety-two, with blue eyes
and ear-length grey hair. Raven's believed to be wearing a
grey or blue jacket, jeans and tennis-shoes. Officers are advised that Code Three applies. Any sighting of this individ-

ual should be reported to Deputy-Director Garrido at Lisbon Central."

It was Raven's last cigarette. "What is Code Three?"

Duncan reached out, silencing the set. "You're probably armed and dangerous."

They climbed back through the one-way system. A spring mechanism closed the glass door behind the two men. The room upstairs stank of cannabis. Duncan opened the French windows again.

"I'm trying to think of the best way of approaching Garrido."

Raven took a long drag on his cigarette. "Do you know him?"

"I know him." The Canadian sat down at his table, locking his hands behind his head. "He's a white Angolan who arrived on the scene just after the revolution. He used to be in army-intelligence. Does the name 'Mesquita' mean anything to you?"

Raven searched his memory uselessly. "No!"

Duncan tilted his chair, maintaining an even keel with one foot. "It happened last year. Two sisters, eighteen and twenty, students at Coimbra University. Their bodies were found in a park, raped and their throats cut. It caused a sensation. The girls' family was ultra-respectable, the father a lawyer in Lisbon. The Coimbra police turned the city inside out. They arrested five suspects and got exactly nowhere. Enter Rui Garrido. It took him two days to nail the culprit, Enrique Mesquita, professor of Oriental studies. He made a full confession in front of the television cameras."

Raven rid himself of his cigarette butt. "And?"

Duncan's foot found the floor again. "He's using a sewing-machine out in the Santa Maria Asylum for the Criminally Insane. We did a four-page spread on it. Garrido got a promotion. I got an award." He nodded at the frame on the wall.

Duncan continued. "Garrido jumped a whole line of people who were senior to him and landed the job he has now, Deputy-Director of the Criminal Police. The one thing we have going for us is that Garrido makes his own rules. The fact that he's put himself in charge of this one means that his nose is twitching."

The picture did little for Raven's confidence. "I don't know why you're telling me all this. It doesn't sound too good to me."

"It's a matter of acting quickly," said Duncan. "You're in a lot better shape than you were a couple of hours ago. You've got me in your corner, for one thing. I can get in to see Garrido."

"And what are you going to say to him?" asked Raven.

Duncan smiled. "The truth. You're a friend of a friend who called me out of the blue, a foreigner who's been framed and is in need of help. We've already got something to back up your story. The trick is to convince Garrido before he turns the key on you. That's the one thing we can't afford to have happen. Once you're in the machinery, it'll take a long time to get you out."

A scrap of paper lifted on the terrace outside and sailed over the parapet. Raven followed it as far as he could with his eyes.

"Is there any chance of getting something to eat?"

"Sure," said Duncan. "But I have to know first what you want me to do. We can turn you in now, let me see what I can do from the street, or we can play my hunch, which is to see Garrido alone and try to work out some sort of a deal."

"I'll go along with the hunch," said Raven. "I wouldn't be a lot of good locked up in jail. I don't have the temperament."

"Fair enough!" Duncan consulted his watch, pulling one of the phones across the table. "I'm going to call my managing editor."

He gave his wink as he waited for the connection to be

made. "This is Cam Duncan in Lisbon," he announced. "Dan Thackeray, please! Dan? Look, I'm onto something really big. I'll try to spell it out for you. An innocent guy framed for murder, cloak-and-dagger agents from the wrong side of the Curtain, and a great deal of money involved. That's it, right here in Lisbon! It's a story that'll run your sales figures off the chart."

He held the receiver away from his ear, rolling his eyes at Raven. "No, I can*not* be more specific. Not at this juncture, anyway. You'll just have to wait a few days. All I need is the green light, Dan. No unauthorized expenditure, that's understood. Nothing that's going to stampede the stockholders. Thanks a lot, feller. You're a prince among men as well as a smart managing editor."

He put the phone back on the rest and looked across the table. "I'll get you some food. There's a restaurant we use at the top of the steps. What do you fancy eating?"

"A steak," said Raven. "Well done, with a salad, if that's OK."

Duncan came to his feet. "You've got it. If you want to call your wife while I'm out, help yourself."

Raven shook his head. He would have given a lot to hear Kirstie's voice, but he lacked the courage to make the call. He watched from the terrace as the Canadian climbed the steps opposite. They were set between leaning houses and hung with iron baskets full of flowers. Duncan was back in twenty minutes, carrying a tray that he placed on the table with a flourish.

"One well-done steak with a tossed salad, compliments of the Toronto *Inquirer*." He patted the back of his chair invitingly.

Raven sat down, stomach juices churning. A carafe of red wine came with the meal.

"I just remembered something," he said. "Ilona Szechenyi's got your telephone number at home. I gave it to her before I knew what was happening."

Duncan was unmoved by the news. "She couldn't have been in touch or Gaby would have told me. She knows where I am."

He phoned again. The conversation was in Portuguese, with Raven catching no more than a word here and there. Duncan cradled the handset.

"Garrido will see me now. Are you sure you'll be all right here on your own?"

Raven shrugged. "Food, wine. What more do I need?"

Duncan grinned. "I think I detect a note of sarcasm. Anyway, I'll leave you to it. I've no idea how long I'll be, but stay where you are. If the telephone rings, don't answer it." He put the box of grass in his shirt pocket.

A couple of minutes later, the street filled with the ragged roar of the Porsche. His food finished, Raven's quest for a cigarette was automatic. He threw the empty package into the trash-basket. His stomach was satisfied, but his need of a smoke was urgent. He searched the drinks cupboard, the drawers in the other rooms, and found nothing. His eyes returned to the supper tray, the empty plates and wine-carafe. His need was becoming desperate. He straightened out the crumpled paper napkin. The name, address and telephone number of the restaurant were printed across a corner. Maybe he could call them, ask them to send someone over with cigarettes. Duncan had said that he used the place regularly. But how would he make himself understood . . . ?

He walked out onto the penthouse terrace. The street below was deserted. A quick dash up the steps would do it. He could take the tray back with him. What would look more natural, a man working late at the office. He carried the tray to the elevator and pressed the down button, leaving the penthouse floor open. The lobby was silent. He opened the glass entrance door and put the tray down on the pavement outside. He wedged the wadded napkin between the chromed strips on the doors so it held in place against the pull of the closing-arm. He picked up the tray again and climbed the steps. The lights of the restaurant were thirty yards away, the opera-house in total darkness. Something moved as he passed the entrance. There was no need to look twice. A uniformed policeman was smoking in front of the box-office. Raven willed his legs forward, essaying the gait of a man without care, his ears on stalks, waiting for the shout that must surely come. It was a long journey to the refuge behind the restaurant curtains.

A man in a white jacket nodded as Raven put the tray on the bar. Raven could see the cop through a chink in the curtains. The man had moved down the steps and was looking in Raven's direction. The candle-lit tables were full. A baize-covered door at the rear of the restaurant led to the kitchen. Excuses leapt to Raven's mind. The look on the barman's face encouraged none of them.

"*Cigarillos francéses,*" said Raven, pointing at a shelf under the bar mirror. He held up three fingers.

The barman placed three packages of Gitanes and made change. Raven hurried out to the street. The cop had disappeared. Raven lit a smoke, cupping the flame. He went down the steps, scanning each doorway. There was no one to be seen when he finally reached lower level. He crossed the street and pushed the glass door. The lock held firmly. Glancing down, he saw the wedge of paper lying on the carpet inside. He stepped back, staring up at the front of the building. The only lights showing were in the penthouse and the lobby. There was no one there, no way of effecting an entrance. The lobby might as well have been a thousand miles away.

His mind jumped, alive to the hunt but with nowhere to go. He turned smartly and made his way up the steps to the restaurant. At least it was a temporary refuge. He had to get off the streets. The barman showed no surprise at Raven's return. The other guests were engrossed in their own affairs. Raven ordered a coffee. He carried the cup to a seat nearby and sat with his back to the door. He had no illusions about his luck holding. By now, flyers bearing his picture would be coming off the presses to be distributed at frontier posts, railroad stations and bus depots. He had no more than a vague idea of where he was. The drive with Duncan had taken them through a neighbourhood of *fado*-houses and bars, streets that were frequented by tourists. The police would be out in force in the area.

He felt in his pocket for Duncan's home number, remembered Ilona and put the piece of paper back. A cab drew up in front of the restaurant, discharging a couple of late diners. Raven left some coins on the table and caught the cab as the driver was moving off.

"Praca Latino Coelho," said Raven, leaning back hard in his seat.

The cab shot forward, down through the one-way system to Rossio and into the climb to the moated castle. The street twisted back on itself. Bleached sheets hung like ghosts from wires attached to the windows and walls of the houses. There were glimpses of wine-taverns with cool dark interiors. The cab emerged three hundred feet above the city. The roofs below were ugly with television masts. Tugs fussed round an oil-tanker out in the river. A white-painted cruise-ship strung with lights was anchored at a pier near the ferry-docks. The statue of Christ the King soared behind the distant suspension bridge.

Raven paid off the driver. The cab made a U-turn, brake-lights glowing as it began its descent. Raven took stock. The wide-open space was the size of a football pitch and surrounded by spreading plane-trees. Coin-operated telescopes offered a birds-eye view of the city. The space between the trees was thronged with people. Saturday night was the traditional night for the family reunion. Dogs and children scooted between the candy-floss stands and carousels. A short row of Victorian houses faced the river. Next to them was an open-air restaurant, the tables set beneath mulberry-trees. A team of white-jacketed chefs sweated over spluttering braziers. Shirt-sleeved men and shiny-faced women were devouring barbecued chicken with their fingers. In command of the scene was a police truck parked at the end of the plaza. It was eleven o'clock.

Raven crossed the road to where a woman was grilling fish in her doorway. She was plump and bodiced in black with a cap of smooth grey hair.

"Senhor Cameron?" he ventured, keeping one eye on the police truck.

The woman gestured with the palm-leaf fan she was wielding.

The house was the last on the row, its front built flush with the pavement. Steps led up to a porch with two bells. Raven pressed them both. The noise of a party in progress came from the upstairs windows—voices and music, laughter. He bent down and peeped through the mail-flap. An eye met his.

"*Quien e?*" asked a man.

Raven hurried back to the safety of the crowd. The door to Cameron's house opened. A man with a glass in his hand stood at the top of the step. He stayed for a moment then closed the door again. Raven's eyes sought the cruise-ship down by the docks. A red ensign was flying at the stern. He had his passport with him, and money. Maybe he could bribe his way onto the ship or sneak aboard somehow. The thought exploded, leaving him suddenly helpless. He started to wander forlornly, attaching himself to the crowd round the carousel. The smell of hot fat mingled with diesel-fumes. Crudely painted models of monsters slowly revolved to the music of the calliope.

Raven turned his head sharply, hearing the calico-tearing rip of the Porsche. The Canadian was out of the car and into his house before Raven could get to him. Raven pushed his way into the open-air restaurant. The party in Duncan's house was still in progress. If he rang the bell again there was the risk of meeting someone who was leaving. The

garden wall abutted onto the rear of the restaurant, where a
waste of nettles masked a rubbish-tip. Raven was half-way
there when he saw the crew of the police truck—short,
sturdy men in baggy grey uniforms and shiny black holsters
and leggings—drinking beer at the bar.

Raven kept going. The wall was too high to climb without assistance. A crate afforded shaky help. He landed hard
on the other side, jarring his teeth and ankles. A dog barked
close by. He picked himself up, stepped over the flower-
bed, and tapped on the window. Duncan pulled the curtain
back. He jerked a thumb and opened a door, hustling Raven
into a large room top-heavy with chintz-covered furniture.
The tone was one of elegant disorder. Books and magazines
were lodged in strange places as if dropped there by people
with a sudden loss of interest. Cigarette-ends had found
their way into a large silver bowl of *pot-pourri*. A bronze of
a Lusitano stallion stood on a Yamaha grand piano. The carpet was old and threadbare. Standing by the open fireplace
was a younger version of Jane Fonda. Her tobacco-brown
hair was cut short, and she was wearing jeans and a man's
shirt with the tails tied across her bare brown stomach.

"This is Gaby, my wife," Duncan said quickly. "The elusive Mr. Raven! Where the hell have you been?"

His wife's handshake was friendly, her eyes curious. "Did
you ring the doorbell about half an hour ago?" Her accent
was language-school English with Canadian vowel sounds.

"That was me," admitted Raven.

"I was in the bath," said Gaby. "Someone upstairs answered."

"The thing is that you're here," said Duncan. He stepped
over a small, square dog with hair the colour and texture of
coconut fibre. The dog curled its lip warningly.

"Patrick telephoned earlier," Gaby added. "He and your
wife are booked on the first flight tomorrow. They get in at
ten past eleven."

"And you all sleep here," said Duncan, producing a bottle

and glasses. "Gaby has the bed ready. I brought your bags from the office. I didn't know what the hell to think when I found you gone. I'd just set up a meeting with Garrido and presto, no Raven!"

Raven circled the dog, taking his drink to the sofa. "When is the meeting?"

"Now," said Duncan. "He's waiting for us."

"Does he speak any English?" asked Raven.

The Canadian nodded from the fireplace. The dog growled as footsteps pounded in the doorway. Duncan looked at his watch.

"They're breaking up early. It isn't even midnight."

Gaby joined Raven on the sofa, a tangle of knitting-wool in her lap. "Your wife was very upset that you hadn't telephoned."

Raven put his glass on the floor. "There wasn't a lot I could say. I mean, nothing that would have put her mind at rest."

"You don't know women," she said quietly.

Her husband's voice was impatient. "Who the hell does? Look, I spent nearly an hour with Garrido. It seems he already knows a hell of a lot more than we thought. For one thing he knows about the money. He's got the newspaper clippings there at the station. And he also knows that Ilona was in the Clínica Galvez. Are you ready?"

Raven came to his feet. Gaby's fingers were flying, weaving the tangled wool into a skein.

"Have you any idea when you'll be back?" she said to her husband.

"I don't have a clue," Duncan answered. "Go to bed."

"I think I will," she said, coming to her feet and kissing him. She smiled at Raven. "He's a monster. But he's a good man to have on your side."

The dog followed her up the stairs. Duncan took a Nikon 35 from a closet. Raven came to his feet.

"Why do I get the impression that you're enjoying all this?"

Duncan switched off the lights and locked the passage to the kitchen. "I guess the answer is that we're a lot alike. If the roles were reversed, *you'd* be enjoying yourself."

The plaza was deserted, the police truck gone, the carousels silent. Waiters were stacking tables in the restaurant next door. But Lisbon was still awake, its seven hills strung with lights. What Raven wanted to do was close his eyes and be transported back to the houseboat, to reach out and touch his wife, see the slow smile break on her face.

"Let's go," said Duncan, breaking the spell.

Rossio was lively, the pavements crowded. The Canadian rammed the Porsche up a street as steep as a ski-run and stopped on a small square dominated by a floodlit pink church. Facing the church was a stone building with steel-shuttered windows and gun emplacements. Radio and television masts spiked the roof.

Duncan nodded back at the church. "It's the only one in the country dedicated to St. Jude. I always think it's a nice touch, the patron of lost causes and police headquarters opposite one another."

A black Mercedes was parked outside the stone building. A silhouette showed behind the steering-wheel.

"Garrido's car," said Duncan. He pulled a joint from his tin and lit it. "A quick toke before we face the music." He inhaled deeply, locking the smoke in his lungs three times before dropping the roach in the street.

"Look," Raven said nervously. "If anything goes wrong, I want you to call the British consul."

"Bullshit," said Duncan. "You'll be out of there before the consul has his eggs and bacon. Try to get a hold on yourself. Remember who you are, a guy with an easy conscience!"

CHAPTER 9

Gotsek was sitting on the balcony, the bedroom behind him in darkness. The lights of the traffic below silhouetted the plane-trees that separated the avenue from the pavements. Gotsek saw none of it. His mind dwelt on more important matters. He had never had the time or desire to form friendships. His emotional needs were wrapped up in music. It had been like this since childhood. But he did know his enemies and Solti was one of them. A man in Gotsek's position was always the object of jealousy, yet recent events had combined in his favour. In fact, what had happened over the last few days might have been designed to further his ultimate triumph. It was like an old-fashioned movie serial with the girl in the snake-pit awaiting the arrival of the sword-wielding hero. Everything hung upon Szechenyi's answer and Gotsek already knew what it would be.

He had started his plan six weeks before, sitting at his piano, the telephone off the hook. He had just left the ministry after his briefing for the Szechenyi mission, hiding his mounting excitement behind the mask that his colleagues had come to know. The plan he'd made then remained unchanged. He had opened the account on his way through Zurich in a small private bank on the Bärengasse. He had sat in an office overlooking the river, facing a man with few illusions about money. The story Gotsek told was essentially the truth. The production of his diplomatic passport made it unassailable. He was, he declared, on a mission of great delicacy, a mission that would result in the transfer of considerable funds to the account he had just opened. There was no doubt in his mind that the banker knew exactly what Gotsek was talking about. The indications were all too obvious. Herr Schaeffli showed no surprise, contenting himself with the details that Gotsek supplied and a signature. The interview lasted less than twenty minutes.

Gotsek groped in his pocket, smiling as he lit the cigarette. He had prepared well over the years, accepting whatever people said about him, the sly smiles as he passed through the typing pool. He had acquired a reputation as a man of patience and guile but one with no personal ambition. A man who could be relied upon to serve his country without thought of gain. His fondness for the good life, the trappings of capitalist decadence, were written off as an acceptable idiosyncrasy, a minor debit on the balance sheet of his overall performance.

He stretched his arms as he thought about the coming meeting with Szechenyi. He intended to make it for tomorrow, here in the city, with his bag already packed. He was booked on the afternoon flight for Zurich. His bank opened at eight o'clock. An hour would be enough to effect the transfer. He'd be in Paris by noon. A Honduran passport awaited him there. It bore his picture and was issued in the name of Juan Bloch, Impresario. The description appealed to him. He had learned the power of money. His safety would be assured, and the musical treasures of the world would be open to him.

He frowned as the telephone rang in the bedroom. It was Nylasi, speaking in Hungarian.

"You had better get over here at once. It's urgent."

Gotsek looked at the travelling clock. "Have you any idea what time it is? It's almost midnight."

"You must come here at once," said Nylasi.

Gotsek sighed. "I'll be there as soon as I can."

The wave of apprehension subsided as he gave himself time to reason. There *could* be no cause for concern. It was surely too late for an enemy to reach him. He went downstairs and surrendered his key at the reception-desk. Then he took the elevator down to the underground garage. He drove using no more than sidelights, checking the rear-view mirror from force of habit. The street that housed the trade delegation was even quieter by night. Boxes containing jars of pickles were stacked in the hallway. Nylasi closed the door hurriedly. Ottilio rose from a chair as the two men came into the room.

"Szechenyi is dead," said Nylasi, wedging his big buttocks into his chair. There was a suggestion of complacency as he looked across at Ottilio. "Tell the counselor exactly what happened."

Ottilio winced and sat down again. Nylasi seemed to find it amusing.

"He fell off his bike. The police were chasing him."

"It wasn't my fault." Ottilio's eyes were on Gotsek. "I did what you told me to do. It wasn't my fault, I swear it."

Nylasi waved impatiently. "Just get on with the story."

"It was light when I got to the villa and I had to be careful that nobody saw me. The machine was no problem. I left it in the trees and worked my way round to the back of the house. There's a little rise there, you get a good view. The Volkswagen was in the carport, and I could see two people in the house, the old man and his daughter."

Nylasi belched and clutched at his breastbone. "There was no sign of the Englishman at this time."

"I stayed where I was," Ottilio continued. "I could see just about everything except for the rooms on the patio side of the house. The old man was drinking and carrying on, staggering around with a bottle, ranting and raving. His daughter kept following him from room to room. I could hear them shouting at one another. That's when Szechenyi fell down. She managed to get him onto the bed in her room. He was in pretty bad shape by then."

"Ottilio's nervous," smiled Nylasi. "He's had a bad time."

There was no doubt about the change in his manner towards Gotsek.

Ottilio wiped his lips. "It was starting to get dark. The sun had already gone down. The girl had moved round to the other side of the house. I heard a car coming through the trees. Then I saw the headlamps. It was the Englishman. He went into the kitchen with the girl. I could hear them talking, but it was in a foreign language. They were there for about ten minutes. He suddenly got up and left the room. Next thing I knew, he was walking towards the car with a couple of suitcases. That's when I heard the shot."

"What shot was that?" Gotsek's brain was still stunned by what he was hearing.

"It came from the girl's bedroom. I could see the Englishman creeping along the wall. He was watching her and I was watching him. She was on the phone, talking to the police, saying that there'd been an argument and the Englishman had shot her father. He'd already taken off by then."

The implications of the disaster that had suddenly engulfed him were becoming all too plain to Gotsek. He turned to Nylasi.

"How many people know about this?"

Nylasi's face bore an expression of implausible regret. "I judged it my duty to inform Budapest. They sent a message back for you. I'll give it to you later."

"You didn't actually see the shot fired?" Gotsek asked Ottilio.

"I didn't have to see the shot fired to know what happened. There were only two people inside the house, the girl and her father, and he was out for the count."

Nylasi's eyes were sly. "The police are looking for the Englishman. They've broadcast his name and description."

Gotsek made his last challenge. "How do you know that Szechenyi is dead?"

Ottilio shrugged. "I have seen dead men. This one had a hole plumb in the middle of his forehead. Just as soon as the Englishman took off, the girl was out on the patio burning a pair of rubber gloves on the brazier. She buried the gun in a flower-bed."

"Get to the point. The counselor's a busy man," Nylasi said sarcastically.

Ottilio screwed up his face, concentrating. "She was walking about the house going from room to room, smoking like a furnace. It must have been a good half-hour before the ambulance arrived with a carload of cops. They loaded the body into the ambulance, then somebody must have seen or heard me. Next thing I knew, they were shining their headlamps through the trees. I managed to get on my bike and called the director from Sintra."

Nylasi struggled up and put an arm around the younger man's shoulders. "You can go on home now."

Ottilio spoke from the doorway. "I want you to know that I did my best," he said to Gotsek.

"The counselor knows that," Nylasi said heartily. "Go on home. I'll talk to you tomorrow morning."

He closed the street door and came back into his office. He opened a drawer and placed a piece of paper on Gotsek's knee. It was a decoded telex message addressed to Gotsek and consisted of five words.

MISSION TERMINATED STOP RETURN FORTHWITH

"I'm very sorry," Nylasi said blandly. "But it isn't the end. I'm sure that your talents will be put to good use. Incidentally, I read the book you recommended by Kafka. Excellent!"

Gotsek wadded the telex message. "I shall remember you," he said, looking the other man full in the face.

"I have no doubt," said Nylasi. "Have a safe journey home."

Gotsek left the rented car in the subterranean garage, the

ignition keys in the lock. He bought himself a large brandy at the bar and carried it upstairs to his room. This was no simple failure, a matter for a transfer to a desk job. This was much graver. He knew how Security worked. They would backtrack carefully until they finally found what they wanted. They wouldn't need proof, just a chink in the curtain, a hint of his intended defection. They'd find that easily enough either in Zurich or Paris. Once that happened, he would join the ranks of the living dead. Without the protection of money, they would find him wherever he went. He walked across to the telephone and called TAP. A girl on night shift took the call. He spoke with the voice of a stranger.

"I'd like a seat on the plane to Budapest tomorrow. I already have the ticket. Nicholas Gotsek."

"That'll be all right, sir," she replied after a moment. "They'll validate your ticket at the airport. Check in no later than a quarter to ten please."

He ripped up his ticket to Zurich and destroyed the bank papers. It was strange. He lacked the courage to kill himself, yet what he was doing amounted to suicide. He undressed and sat on the side of the bed, looking at the phone in the darkness. There wasn't a single soul alive who would answer his call for help.

CHAPTER 10

They crossed the square, their journey watched by the man sitting at the wheel of the Mercedes. An armed policeman barred their way at the top of the steps. Duncan said something in Portuguese and the man led them along a passageway. The scene was remote from Raven's experience. There was none of the Saturday-night bustle of a British police station, nothing but closed doors and forbidding corridors. The policeman rapped on a door and vanished.

A slightly built man rose behind a desk. His pale face was deeply slashed with lines and he had the eyes of an inquisitor. He was wearing baggy tan trousers and a bush jacket.

"Deputy-Director Garrido," said Duncan in English. "Mr. Raven speaks no Portuguese."

The official's reaction was brusque. "Empty your pockets, please," he said. "Place everything on the desk."

He watched narrowly, making two separate piles of the objects that Raven removed. Passport, papers and flight ticket went on one side, money and keys on the other. Duncan sprawled on a chair, eyes on the ceiling, whistling tonelessly.

Garrido came round the desk. "Put your hands on the wall and make your legs wide."

Raven assumed the required position. His reception was far from what he had expected. Garrido's search was deft. His hands ran the length of Raven's body, feeling the back of his neck, his armpits and groin.

"Take off your socks and shoes," he ordered. He banged each sneaker against the wall and shook out the socks.

Raven retied his shoelaces. "Is it all right if I smoke?"

Garrido pushed a pack of cigarettes across the desk. An ashtray followed. "How long have you two known one another?"

Raven used his lighter. "He's a friend of my lawyer in England. That's where we met."

Garrido glanced at a sheet of paper. "Your lawyer's name is Patrick O'Callaghan?"

"That's right," said Raven.

"And your wife, how long have you known her?"

"My *wife?*" Raven repeated. "You're asking me how long I've known my wife? I don't get the connection."

Garrido's tone was firm but courteous. "Just answer my questions, please. And I must tell you that what we are saying is being recorded. There is fair play here like in England."

"Answer his question," said Duncan.

"About four years," said Raven. "We were married last October."

Garrido brooded, his hands folded in front of him. The backs of his fingers were covered with coarse black hair. He brought his head up.

"Why did you run from the Vila Verde?"

"Why did I run? I'd have thought that was obvious. A man had been killed and his daughter was saying that I had done it."

Garrido shook his head. "The lady reported an accident. She said there had been a struggle and that the gun went off. She could not believe that you meant to kill her father."

"That's what she said, is it?" Raven asked quietly.

"There was an argument about money and a signet-ring. Her father was dead when she came into the room."

"There was no argument," Raven burst out. "The woman's a liar. She's sick in the head as well."

Garrido waved a hand. "You have been a policeman, Senhor Raven. An innocent man does not flee. I am sure you know that. I told you, there is fair play in Portugal. How about the way I am treating you now?"

"I've no complaints," answered Raven. Someone along the corridor was shouting his head off.

"Where is your wife?" Garrido went on.

Raven was getting tired of it. "You know very well where she is."

"I prefer you to tell me," said Garrido.

"OK, she's in England. She had to go back on a job. She's a professional photographer."

Garrido unfolded a telex message he had taken from a drawer. "Freelance photographer?"

"That's right. Look, I didn't know *any* of these people until three weeks ago. My wife was at school with Ilona Szechenyi. That's how we came to be here. Some holiday."

Garrido put his finger on the telex form. "This is from England, from the Commissioner of the Metropolitan Police. I wouldn't call it a very good reference."

"I wouldn't expect it to be," said Raven. It was no trick to guess the contents.

"Why did you retire from the police, Senhor Raven?"

Raven shot a quick look at Duncan. There was no help from that direction. The Canadian was lost in thoughts of his own.

"It's a long story," said Raven. "Call it a conflict of personalities. You're in the same line of business. You know the way things go. Or you know the way things *can* go."

Garrido's hand snaked across the desk. He opened Raven's passport and held the pages against the light from the angle-poise lamp. He applied the same care to a study of the credit cards.

"What job do you do now?" he asked, putting the credit cards back in their plastic case.

"I don't do anything." The admission sounded damaging even to his own ears. Raven tried to explain. "I have enough money to live on, family money."

Garrido leaned forward on his elbows. The movement revealed that hairs grew on his throat as well as on the back of his hands.

"You were deported from France?"

"Wrong for a start," Raven said promptly. "The authorities asked me to leave. There's a difference. In any case, it was all a misunderstanding. I go to France regularly. We have an apartment in Paris." He had a feeling that he was not doing well, and they had barely touched on the subject at issue.

The deputy-director's eyes sought the paper in front of him. "'An exemplary service record marred by indiscipline,'" he quoted. "What does this mean?"

Raven did his best with the little he had. "I had a reputation for doing things in my own way, cutting corners, if you like. It's cost me a lot, but there's nothing I can do about it. It's the way that I am. I can't *be* any other way."

"Come on now, Rui," Duncan broke in impatiently. "Stop giving the guy a hard time. You promised to hear him out. All this other stuff's pointless."

Noise of a scuffle sounded along the corridor. Garrido went to the door and shouted. The noise ceased abruptly. The deputy-director resumed his seat.

"Why don't *you* tell me what happened?"

Raven pulled himself together. "There are things that you have to understand. Like Gotsek, for instance. Do you know about Gotsek?"

"It is not important what you think I know," said Garrido. "It is important what you tell me."

The Canadian's feet scraped the floor. "Tell him, for crissakes!"

It was twenty minutes to one when Raven started talking, ten past by the time he had finished. He had to score an A for effort in spite of the gaps in his story. Telling it, he was conscious that there were too many skeletons in need of fleshing out. Neither Garrido nor Duncan made any comment. The policeman's eyes remained where they had been for the last half-hour, fixed firmly on Raven's face.

Raven lifted his hands, a gesture of supplication, he wasn't sure. Neither of these people really understood.

"Things just got out of hand," he said defensively.

"There is a lot that needs explanation," Garrido answered quietly. "The weapon, for instance."

"The weapon," Raven repeated, blinking.

Garrido sifted through his pile of papers. "A five-shot thirty-two calibre revolver registered in the name of Stephen Szechenyi. His daughter says that you took this weapon with you when you fled."

"What do you expect her to say?" put in Duncan. "This guy's got no gun."

"And the signet-ring," Garrido continued. "She says you took that too."

"I don't believe this!" Raven said, appealing to both of them. "This woman is turning things round completely. What use would the ring have been to me? I'd already made up my mind to go back to England. I'd had enough of the Szechenyis."

Garrido slipped his papers back in the drawer, his lined face serious. "You already knew the account number. The transfer was in your possession. You needed the signet-ring."

The suggestion stung Raven to anger. "Are you out of your mind? Don't you realize that this is no run-of-the-mill liar! The woman's sick but she's cunning and devious. I'm the only person who knows the truth about her. She's *got* to destroy me!"

Garrido moved a hand from side to side like a priest bestowing a blessing. "Criminals are not allowed to profit from their transgressions. This is the law in Portugal."

Duncan sprang to life. "What about the abduction?"

Garrido's face cracked open like a ventriloquist's dummy. "I know nothing of any abduction except from you."

The other two raced to reply. Duncan got there first. "OK, how about the key that she stole, the statement of the building superintendent?"

Garrido shook his head, clicking his tongue. "Impersonating police-officers." He barely smiled, but it was a movement in the right direction.

"Senhor Gotsek," he announced. "An official of the Hungarian Foreign Ministry with a diplomatic passport, an individual who is not to be questioned."

Raven felt like a man trapped in a swamp. "What are you people doing to me?" he shouted.

Duncan waved him to silence. He leaned forward, pointing at the policeman. "You're going to have to do better than this, Rui!" He switched to Portuguese.

Raven was silent as the other two argued.

"It's not his fault," Duncan explained when they had finished. "It's the people at the Ministry of Justice. They're scared shitless of having Gotsek questioned."

"So what are they going to do with him?" Raven asked bitterly. "Put him up for canonization?"

"Have you ever heard of the Mathieson test?" Duncan hung on the answer.

"Of course I've heard of it. It shows if you've fired a hand-gun recently."

"Ilona Szechenyi's already taken it. The result was negative."

"You mean that she's been here?" asked Raven.

"Apparently yes. She left three quarters of an hour ago. The deputy-director wants to know whether you're willing to take the test."

"This is an investigation into a murder," Garrido said calmly. "The lady was co-operative."

"*Co-operative?*" Raven gagged on the word. He turned to Duncan in desperation. "She's got him conned too! *She was wearing rubber gloves!*"

"You are willing to take the test?" asked Garrido.

"Any time, any place," said Raven, aware that he was making a fool of himself yet unable to do anything about it.

"Come with me, please," said Garrido, rising. "Both of you!"

There were smears of blood on the corridor walls, red snail trails where fingers had found momentary hold. Garrido went first, opening and shutting a succession of doors until they finally reached a laboratory. Garrido switched on the overhead lights. Steel shutters covered the windows. Zinc-lined sinks ran down the center of the room with workbenches on either side. Shelves held glass jars and drums of chemicals, and there was a strong smell of gas.

The deputy-director lit a bunsen burner and adjusted the flame. He broke a segment of paraffin wax into an iron pot and placed it on the burner.

"Pull up your sleeve!" he said to Raven. He dipped a glass rod into the melted wax, testing its consistency on the back of his fingers. He held Raven's right hand over the sink and covered it with wax to the wrist. The wax clung warm to the skin, the hairs stiffening as it cooled. Garrido moved Raven to the bench, still supporting his arm. Satisfied that the wax had set, he drew a blunt-edged knife along the inside of Raven's wrist, then down across the palm to the middle finger. He peeled off the divided cast and laid it gently on a bed of blotting-paper.

Raven picked the last shreds of wax from his skin. The test was standard. A puff of gas followed a spent shell ejected from a gun, depositing cordite residue on the index and second fingers. Garrido dipped the glass rod into a solution and tried it on the cast. He bent, watching intently, as the wax turned blue. He dropped the cast in the trashbasket and took Raven's other arm.

"It is possible you are left-handed."

Duncan was showing little interest in the proceedings, amusing himself by sending long licks of flame from the end of the gas jet. Garrido got rid of the second cast and washed his hands at the sink.

"So both tests are negative," he said. For the first time he showed signs of humour. "Perhaps you too wore gloves!"

He cut the lights and led them back along the echoing corridors. He stopped in front of his door, signalling Raven to go in while detaining the Canadian outside. Raven could hear them arguing. They came in, avoiding looking in Raven's direction.

"I'm sorry," said Duncan. "He's decided to hold you for the examining magistrate."

Garrido spread his hands. "You must understand my dilemma. A man in the morgue is certainly dead. The stories accounting for his death are directly in conflict."

Raven sat down slowly. "I've already told you that this woman's a liar. I've *proved* it, for crissakes! And you're holding me on her word alone."

"You'll regret this, Rui," warned Duncan. "I'll take good care that you regret it."

Garrido ignored him, addressing himself to Raven. "You are a visitor to this country. Portugal and England are the oldest allies known. We have learned from one another through the years. But what have you done here, eh? Serious crimes are committed. You know about this but say nothing. Senhor John Raven, the ex-Inspector-Detective, says nothing. You show no respect for the law."

Raven whacked his fist on his knee. "But that's absolute nonsense! I tried to get Szechenyi to go to the police. I must have said it half a dozen times. If he'd listened to me, he'd still be alive."

Duncan produced a joint from his tin box and lit it deliberately. "I've been good to you," he said to Garrido. "I've protected your ass in polite society. It's because of me that you're deputy-director. Three thousand words of prolonged applause. You simply cannot do this to me."

Garrido raised his arms. "The examining magistrate must decide."

"The examining magistrate!" Duncan's face clouded. "You'll be holding Raven on a charge of murder, and I know what that means. Once you've got him in your cells, it'll take an act of parliament to get him out. Any magistrate is going to have a field day with this one."

"I promised I would listen," Garrido said calmly. "I have listened."

Duncan made one last effort. "This isn't a threat, Rui. We know one another too well for that. But a lot of important people are going to be asking questions. You've got John's passport. His wife and his lawyer will be here in just a few hours' time. Parole him in my custody. I give you my word he won't run!"

"I'm sorry," Garrido said unyieldingly.

Raven looked up, seeing the months stretching ahead, Kirstie dragging herself to visit some stinking jail. He came to his feet, facing the policeman, his voice shaking.

"You want the truth! OK, I'll give you the truth if only you'll do what I say!" He began to talk fast, despair adding force to his pleading.

Garrido listened intently. Duncan continued to smoke, his eyes half-closed.

"*Basta!*" said Garrido when Raven had done. He looked from his watch to the Canadian. "You are my witness that this man has made a request. There is no compulsion from me."

"No compulsion," said Duncan, opening his eyes. "You want a statement to that effect, you've got it."

Duncan came to life as Garrido left the room. "You're sure you can handle this?"

"If he gives me the chance," said Raven. The adrenalin was running and there was no thought of failure.

Duncan killed his smoke in the ashtray and winked a lazy

eye. "He'll give you the chance, all right. That was a stroke of genius, what you just said. You managed to hit on the one thing that would grab him."

"It has to be done my way," said Raven, listening for the policeman's return. "If she as much as sniffs police, then I've had it. I've got to come on as the guy with nowhere to go, the fugitive pleading for his life."

"She might well blow your brains asunder," said Duncan.

The thought had already occurred to him, but it was a chance that Raven would take. "What you have to do is convince Garrido that she's as quick as a rattlesnake and twice as dangerous. One wrong word, the least hint of something she knows shouldn't be there . . ." He drew his finger across his windpipe.

Duncan's voice was reassuring. "Garrido's treading on eggs. That stuff about people asking questions had him worried, I could tell. I'm not sure he knows what he wants. Handing you over to the examining magistrate could blow up in his face, but he can't bring himself to turn you loose. If you can deliver this bitch, Garrido's going to claim the idea as his own. I can see him now, showing his footwork to the local press."

The deputy-director came through the door carrying a dispatch-case. He opened it on the desk, displaying an elaborate control panel. Both men jumped as Garrido's voice bellowed from concealed speakers. Garrido revealed the quartz watch in his hand.

"Jesus Christ!" said Duncan, shaking his head. "You almost broke my ear-drum."

"Japanese," Garrido said with satisfaction. "I have obtained the best results with this machine. Give me your watch, please," he added, extending a hand to Raven.

Raven exchanged his Omega for the Quartz wrist-watch. A button by the winder-stem activated a tiny microphone in the case.

"On, off," Garrido demonstrated. "Now you try!"

Raven sent his voice through the speakers. "One, two, three, four . . ." A sudden thought sparked the query. "What sort of range does it have?"

"It'll carry a mile," said Duncan. "We use them all the time in the business. The sound's good and you get a clear recording. He knows what he's doing."

Garrido smiled. The introduction of electronics had completely transformed him. There was almost a sense of camaraderie now between the three men. The policeman passed a typewritten sheet of paper across the desk. There was space for two signatures at the bottom. Duncan translated.

"It says that you're doing this of your own free-will and that nobody pressured you. He wants an out if something goes wrong."

Raven wrote his name with the distinct impression that his face had paled visibly. Duncan added his own scrawl and grinned happily.

"I feel like I was twenty years old, off to bang some broad who's my social superior."

"You're stoned," said Raven. He turned to Garrido. "I'm dead if she knows what's happening."

Garrido's look was superior. "You must not worry. There is nothing to fear except what is in your head."

A smile lingered on his face as he turned off the lights. A young man joined them at the end of the corridor. He was wearing a Rolling Stones T-shirt and a police-special thrust down the front of his jeans. He travelled with Garrido and the driver in the Mercedes. The Porsche led the way.

Duncan fastened his seat-belt. "We're in this together, right? Two righteous citizens set apart by fate but with hearts that beat in unison."

"You'd better let me drive," said Raven. "You're out of your skull."

Duncan turned the ignition key. "You're right as it happens, old buddy, but I can still outdrive the rest of you."

The two cars left the city with dimmed headlamps. It was

twenty minutes past three by the clock in the Central Post Office. Strobes blinked on empty pavements. Duncan was as good as his word, wheeling the Porsche like a rally driver. The Mercedes maintained its distance behind. They were out on the Estoril highway by now and travelling fast. Raven reached for a cigarette. They would have to stop well clear of the villa. The picture of Ilona asleep in her bed eluded him. He imagined her sitting fully dressed by the window, protected by some sixth sense that would warn her of his return.

He stuck his hand through the open window, pointing at the northbound exit from the motorway. The lights of Sintra showed in front of them. The two cars went into the long ascent, wipers swishing as they ran through the belt of sea fog. Then they were over the mountain, with stubbled fields stretching away on each side. Vineyards flashed by, a cluster of bone-white cottages, a river overhung by willow-trees. Raven leaned forward, peering through the windshield as they approached the bend.

"Slow down!" he said sharply.

Duncan touched the brake-pedal, bringing the Porsche to a halt. The sandy track leading to the villa glimmered in the pine-trees. The silence was complete now that both cars had stopped. Duncan unfastened his seat-belt, cocking his head at Raven.

"You're sure you want to go through with this?"

Garrido was walking towards them. "It's too late for anything else," said Raven.

The Canadian shrugged. The drive appeared to have sobered him. "You do what you have to, friend. Whatever happens, I'm right behind you."

Raven started taking his sneakers and socks off. He placed them on the jump seat behind. "Do you know where the villa is?" Garrido was leaning through the open window.

"No," said Garrido. "I did not come when we fetched her."

Raven explained the layout. "I don't want you people moving about. Stay in the car and keep your ears open. You're sure that this thing's going to work?"

"It'll work," Duncan said quietly.

Raven picked his way across last year's pine-needles. He touched the button on the watch, activating the microphone. He left the track for the shelter of the trees, working his way towards the beach. Branches reached out, snagging his shirt and jeans.

He slithered down the dunes, avoiding the clumps of sea holly. The sky had brightened perceptibly. The first streaks of dawn tinted the sand. Holding up his arms, he waded out into the water until it reached his knees. Then he turned and headed back towards the villa. He stopped at the wall at the end of the patio and raised his head cautiously. The Volkswagen was parked in the carport; the villa was in darkness. The goldfish swirled as he tiptoed across the patio. He edged along the wall moving sideways as far as Ilona's bedroom. He peeped through the window, holding the billowing curtain to one side. There was enough light to see that the bed had been remade, the blood-stained rug removed. He inched away to the kitchen end of the house and squatted by the wall. His jeans were soaked, his shirt ripped in places. He turned his wrist, squinting down at the jerking second hand. The tiny button was still depressed, linking him to the tape that should be recording each sound that he made. It was twenty minutes to four, with the sky growing lighter by the minute.

He bent his head impulsively, bringing his mouth close to the watch-face. "If you're there," he whispered. "I'm going inside."

He padded across the flagstones and rattled the French doors. "Ilona?"

There was no response. His fingers closed on the handle. The doors were open. He pushed the curtain aside and stepped forward into warm darkness.

The light came on suddenly, blinding him. When his eyes refocused, he saw Ilona Szechenyi standing at the end of the corridor, her hair loose on her shoulders and clad in her night-dress. She was holding the gun with two hands, the barrel trained on Raven's stomach.

He opened his mouth but no words came. His next effort produced a hoarse rattle.

Her eyes travelled down his body to his bare feet. "Where are your shoes?"

He lowered his arms cautiously. The watch on his wrist felt the size of an alarm clock.

"I've been in the water," he said. "I had to talk to you."

She moved the gun a fraction, pointing along the corridor. She followed him into her bedroom, the gun at his back. The tumbled bed in Szechenyi's room showed that she had been lying there. He sat on the stool in front of her dressing-table, his back to the mirror. The floor was littered with exploded flash bulbs that the police must have used.

The flimsy night-dress clung to her body as she spoke. "You're a fool! You should never have come back here."

He built on the hint of regret in her voice. "I had to be sure." The room smelled of her scent.

She lifted the weight of her hair with one hand. Her neck glistened with sweat. Outside, the birds had begun their first chorus.

"You had to be sure about what?" His statement had clearly intrigued her.

The cheval-glass on his left reflected Szechenyi's room. She must have hidden the gun before the police arrived. She came forward slowly and sat on the edge of the bed, her free hand only inches away from the telephone.

"You had to be sure about what?" she repeated.

"Us," he said simply. There was a weird fascination about this half-naked woman with only one thought in her head, the wish to destroy him. This was what he had to prove by the questions he asked and the answers she gave.

She let her hair fall. "Don't you know that the police are looking for you?"

He showed her his cigarettes and lighter and lit a smoke. "Why did you do it, Ilona?"

She glanced sideways, looking at her reflection in the long tilted mirror. "I warned you. You had your chance. Where have you been since then?"

"There were road-blocks all over the place. I ditched the car and started walking back along the beach. It's a long way."

"You're lying," she said. Her eyes were brilliant and restless.

He shook his head, praying that the microphone was working. "I know the truth now, Ilona. You killed Karolyi as well as your father. I've tried to understand why."

"Spare me the moral indignation," she said. "Just light a cigarette and put it on the ashtray. I'll kill you if I have to, John, be very sure about it."

He did as she said, placing the lighted cigarette on the bedside-table between them. Five nickel bullet heads lying on the table showed that the gun had been reloaded.

"They stood in my way as you do now," she said. "I could have loved you, John. Remember that!"

"That's just not true," he replied. Her readiness to kill was established. At a range of six feet she could hardly miss. "You're not capable of loving anyone. You're a sick woman in need of help."

She tinkled a laugh of disdain. "You mean you came back here to tell me that. Nonsense! Not that it matters too much —*now*," she ended significantly.

"You're going to kill me, is that it?" Any moment now she would get the drift, realize the significance of what he was saying.

She answered like a mother who is forced to explain yet again to a child. "I can't let you go, John. It's too late."

He forced a semblance of steadiness into his voice. "Think about the consequences."

"Oh, but I have," she said coolly. "The police aren't looking for me, they're looking for you. I shall tell them that you came back and that you threatened me. They already know we were lovers. I'll say that I promised I'd help you escape, that we went to bed and you woke as I was taking your gun. I killed you in self-defence, John. Poor John." She smiled at him sadly.

He shifted his weight onto his right leg, bringing his body in line with the cheval-mirror. *Garrido, don't fail me now!* Surely they had enough on the tape to start moving.

He continued to play for time. "Kirstie's been your friend for fifteen years. I can't believe that you've no feeling left at all for her."

She offered her sad, sweet smile. "She called half an hour ago. She seems to have things mixed up. We had the whole performance, floods of tears, recriminations and some horrid insinuations. I put the record straight and told her the truth. Oh yes, I have a lot of feeling for Kirstie Macfarlane."

Sudden blind rage took his fear away. "You're evil, Ilona, poisonous. Not fit to live."

She raised the gun slowly, her left hand supporting her right wrist. His foot caught the mirror, toppling it over between them as she fired. Splintered glass covered the front of his body. He hit the floor hard and rolled towards the bed. He could just see her legs as she backed into the corridor. He rolled over again, presenting as small a target as he could. His ears still rang from the explosion, but he could hear the sound of a car outside. A second shot smacked into the wall behind him. The patio doors burst open and suddenly Duncan was shouting Raven's name. Raven staggered out into the corridor. Early morning radiance lit the sitting-room where the Canadian was holding Ilona in a half-nelson. Behind him was Garrido standing in the splintered door-frame with his gun out. The man in the Rolling Stones T-shirt was guarding the way to the kitchen.

Duncan relaxed his grip and Ilona wrenched herself free. She crossed her arms, shielding her nakedness, her husky voice for Raven alone.

"It looks as though I was the fool after all."

Someone must have taken her gun. The splintered glass had bloodied her legs. Raven looked through the doors at the sea rather than look at her face. The chase was over. He had never had much liking for the kill.

"We could have had everything, you and I," she said softly. "Everything in the whole wide world if only you had wanted it."

Duncan hooted behind her. "This has to be the worst dialogue since *Gone With the Wind*. Lock her up, for God's sake."

Ilona ignored him, her voice now barely audible. "What will they do to me, John?"

Raven turned his head slowly. Only her eyes were alive in a face that was otherwise dead.

"I don't know. I'm not sure."

Garrido seized her by the arm. "Please put some clothes on. You are coming with us."

She nodded quickly. Garrido walked her towards the corridor still holding her arm. She stopped as they passed Raven, looking him full in the eye. Her lips pursed, and for a moment he thought she would spit at him. But she smiled instead.

"I love you, John Raven."

His mind was still dealing with the look she had given him when a shot preceded Garrido's shout. By the time Raven reached the bedroom, Ilona was lying on the floor, blood pumping from a blackened hole in her temple. Her right hand still gripped the revolver. The fingers of her left hand opened spasmodically as he watched, releasing Szechenyi's signet-ring. Raven picked it up from the floor and gave it to Garrido.

"You'd better take this."

Garrido walked across the corridor to the phone in Ilona's bedroom. Duncan threw the windows wide, letting the acrid fumes of the explosion drift into the cool of the morning. A cold sweat broke out on Raven's body and he ran for the bathroom. He managed to sink to his knees before retching into the toilet-bowl. His stomach voided, he ran cold water on his head. His dive away from the gunshot earlier had smashed the glass on the wrist-watch. He took it off and left it on the window-ledge.

Garrido was still on the phone, his partner drinking beer in the kitchen. Duncan followed Raven down the corridor. The two men stood by the fish-pond, looking out across the ocean.

"Questions are going to be asked," said the Canadian. "How did she manage to have the gun?"

Raven shrugged, lighting yet another cigarette. Whatever habit was bad, then he had it.

"I don't know. She must have thrown it on the bed as she came out to meet you."

The Canadian stifled a yawn. The sky was a pale-blue bowl with the first fire of the rising sun tingeing the Sintra Mountains. It was a new day after a long night.

Duncan filled his lungs and exhaled noisily. "Garrido's called for an ambulance. Don't look so down, man. There's nothing to reproach yourself for. What happened is just about the best thing for everyone including her, poor bitch. They tell me death wipes the slate clean. We heard the whole thing sitting there in the car."

Raven wiped his fingers surreptitiously. They still smelled of Ilona's scent.

"Did you hear that bit about Kirstie? That she'd called here earlier?"

"I heard," said Duncan. "Don't worry. Things'll work out."

Garrido emerged from the sitting-room holding an envelope. "I found this in her handbag."

Raven recognized the bank-transfer. "You've got it all now," grinned Duncan. "You're a rich man, Rui."

The fish flashed as Raven turned. "Who gets the money now?"

Duncan made a wry face. "Who always gets the money in the end? The banks is who! How about it, Rui. Why don't you tell the guy that he's free, that the case is closed."

"The case is closed." The beard was sprouting dark on Garrido's cheeks. "The problem is Gotsek. I shall be writing reports long after you have forgotten this affair."

"May I say something?" asked Raven. "You won't take offence?"

"Whatever you wish." Garrido glanced at his watch.

"What you just did was what I would have done. It's just what always got me into trouble."

Garrido's smile was totally unexpected. "Rules are for judges, not for policemen. You must excuse me now. I have to go back to the city. No bed for me tonight, or rather today."

Raven dusted the fish-food from his palm. "I'd like to go to the airport. I want to be there when my wife arrives."

"That is entirely up to you," Garrido's mind was clearly on other things. "I shall be at Central should you want me."

"I'll buy us all lunch," said Duncan. "Why don't you join us, Rui?"

Duncan's camera was slung on the back of the garden recliner. Garrido pointed a finger at it.

"You'll take no pictures here, not until we've finished at least."

"Gratitude," said Duncan.

Raven smiled wanly. He was tired and dirty and had

things on his mind. The events of the last few hours had shaken his confidence in himself. *A perverse will to lose* was what Kirstie had said. Maybe she was right after all.

"I left your watch in the bathroom. I'm afraid that it's broken."

Garrido brooded for a moment. "Make the most of your story," he said at last. "I shall not forget your assistance."

He walked away, leaving a slip of folded paper on the glass-topped table. The young cop was still in the villa. Seconds later they heard the Mercedes being started.

Duncan took the slip of paper. "God*dam!*" he cried jubilantly. "That guy's unpredictable. He's given us Gotsek's address! I want to go there, John. I mean *now!*"

Raven shrugged. The time had come to keep his end of the bargain. Sleep no longer mattered.

"If Gotsek knows who you are, he won't see you. If he doesn't know, he still won't see you."

"He'll see you though!" Duncan's sun-tanned face was excited. "He won't be able to resist it."

The cop in the T-shirt watched them leave the premises. They passed the ambulance this side of Sintra, travelling fast and preceded by a police car. Men were at work in the fields, children waiting at the stand-pipes with water containers. Lopsided vegetable trucks crawled in the slow lane. By the time they reached the city, it was eight o'clock and the full glare of the sun was on the windshield. Duncan lowered the visor.

"Let's get some coffee before we go in to see this bastard."

He pulled the Porsche onto the service road flanking the eight-lane Avenida da Liberdade. A bus was drawn up in front of the Hotel Peninsular. Porters were loading baggage into the hold. The two men walked to a nearby café under the trees. Water ran in the gutters, releasing the smell of the flower-beds.

A waiter brought a newspaper with the coffee. Duncan

scanned it hurriedly. "Not a single word!" he announced triumphantly. "Garrido's managed to keep it on the back burner somehow."

"I think we've got company," Raven said quietly. There was a car parked behind the coach, two men in front, two behind.

Duncan turned his head briefly. "No sweat. Just another police car. They fall over themselves. Some kind of security service probably. One thing you can bet on, they're not interested in us."

Raven emptied the sachet of sugar into his cup. "How long have you been married?"

The Canadian's eyebrows made a bridge across the top of his nose. "Four years in November, why?"

Raven sipped the hot strong brew and put the cup down. "Did you ever cheat on your wife?"

A hint of a smile joined the Canadian's frown. "What kind of a question is that?"

"Well, have you?"

Duncan gave it some thought. "A couple of one-night stands. Nothing serious. You know the way it is. A guy gets lonely away from home. Is that what's still bothering you?"

Raven nodded. "It's the first time for me, believe it or not. Not that that's an excuse. In fact, if you asked me why I did it, I wouldn't be able to tell you. I wasn't even drunk."

Two of the men had left the car and were looking in a shop-window. "You think your wife knows about it?" Duncan demanded.

"I'm damn sure that she does." The thought curdled whatever was left in Raven's stomach.

"Deny it!" said Duncan. "Garrido will bury your statement. She'll never know the difference."

It was a tempting idea but one without substance. "We don't lie to one another," said Raven.

Duncan made a face. "Then you're dafter than I thought. What do you think marriage is, 'The Truth Game'? People have to lie sometimes to protect other people. I do and I'm pretty sure that Gaby does. Look your wife straight in the eye and deny it. If she's the kind of woman I take her to be, she'll believe you."

"You don't know Kirstie." Raven shifted his chair away from the running water. "I don't want to lose her, Cam. There's a chance that I won't if I tell her the truth, none at all if I lie to her."

Duncan laid some money on the table. "You won't lose her. Wait until she hears my version. You'll come out ahead of Rob Roy. I'm going to nail this bastard Gotsek. I'm good at my job. People are going to understand that these things can happen."

"And you're modest with it," said Raven. His mouth was dry and dusty. "You could turn me into Sir Galahad. Gotsek didn't screw Ilona. I did."

"You're making heavy weather of it," said Duncan. He snapped a couple of frames of Raven with the police car in the background. "Let's go!"

They waited as a busload of tourists surged from the hotel. The Canadian dropped into an armchair and hid himself behind his newspaper. The desk clerk looked up as Raven neared, his welcoming smile fading somewhat as he noticed the stained and torn clothing.

"May I help you, sir?" he intoned loftily.

"Mr. Gotsek, please."

The clerk scanned a register, his face dubious. "Is the gentleman expecting you?"

"Just call the room," said Raven, "and give him my name." He spelled it for better measure.

The clerk spoke briefly and put the phone down. "The gentleman will see you."

Raven lifted a hand. Duncan joined him at the elevators. They emerged into a corridor partially blocked by laundry-trolleys. Chambermaids were changing bedding in the rooms that had already been vacated.

Raven knocked on a door. "It is open," a voice replied.

Gotsek was standing with his back to the windows, too far away to prevent Duncan's entrance. The Canadian slipped the catch.

Gotsek was younger than Raven expected, with a well-nourished face and reddish hair. He was wearing a silk shirt with a striped flannel suit. A packed Vuitton travelling-bag lay ready on the stand, a passport and airline ticket on the table by the bed.

The Canadian picked up the flight ticket. "Good heavens!" he said with mock astonishment. "Not only is the gentleman a diplomat, he's on his way to Budapest!"

He panned his camera round the room, working the shutter release.

Gotsek moved towards the telephone with surprising speed, but Raven got there first. The Hungarian backed off, his eyes shifting from one to the other.

"Who is this man?" he asked Raven. "What do you people want?"

A maid outside rattled the locked door. Duncan changed the film pack in his camera. "This is Cameron Duncan of the Toronto *Inquirer*," said Raven. "He's doing a feature article on your visit to Portugal."

Gotsek wiped his mouth. His English had the same harsh consonants as Szechenyi's.

"I advise you to be very careful. I represent my government."

Duncan finished the orange juice on the breakfast-table. "Hear that? The People's Republic of Hungary, no less!"

Gotsek's face tightened. "You are unwelcome intruders, both of you. If you will not leave, I shall call for assistance."

For a moment it seemed that he would go to the door. Raven was still guarding the telephone.

"We're on our way," Duncan said cheerfully. "You might like to hear what I intend to print. You, sir, came to this country with one purpose in mind, to blackmail a man out of a fortune that was legally his. You can forget the diplomatic passport. I'm going to show you for what you really are."

"If you don't already know it," said Raven. "Ilona Szechenyi killed her father last night. She shot herself an hour ago."

Gotsek put the flight ticket and passport in his jacket pocket. "You are an enigma to me, Mr. Raven. I am not sure what part you have played in all this, but let me give you some advice. If you are thinking of buying a yacht in the future, be careful when you take on crew."

Duncan's grin was delighted. "Get that, John! Goddammit, man, I always knew you were a wrong 'un!"

"What else?" shrugged Raven. There was real fear behind Gotsek's bluster. "You blew it," Raven said to him. "All these people are dead and the money rolls on forever, property of the Banque Suisse et Ottomane. They're not going to like that at home!"

Duncan slung his camera over his shoulder. "Let me ask you one last question, Counselor. Does the Toronto *Inquirer* sell in your city or shall I send you a copy?"

Gotsek's freckled face tightened. "You are preventing me from using the telephone."

Raven handed the instrument across the bed.

"Room four-one-two," said Gotsek. "I would like a cab to take me to the airport. Send someone up for my bag."

The panama hat that he placed on his head gave him an air of eccentricity. "Now go," he said quietly.

Raven and Duncan made their way down to the street. The Sunday exodus from the city had already started. Convoys of cars headed south and west for the beaches of Cascais and Caparica. Church bells summoned the faithful. Duncan lowered the top of the Porsche and settled himself behind the wheel. The bus had gone but the black car was still there.

"Waiting for Gotsek," said Duncan, grinning.

Raven cleared his throat. He was tired and his legs ached and thoughts floated just out of reach.

"We'd better check in with Garrido."

The doors of the church were wide open. A couple of nuns were shepherding small boys dressed in sailor suits up the steps. The sound of the organ filled the small square. The police building was less grim in the sunshine. A woman was selling flowers outside. Duncan had a word with the cop in the lobby. He accompanied them down the corridor. Raven noticed that the blood-stains had been washed from the walls.

Garrido had shaved and was wearing a suit. A plastic bag on his desk contained the bank-transfer and Szechenyi's signet-ring. The revolver was in another bag. Garrido pushed Raven's belongings across.

"I did not expect to see you as soon as this."

"We had a call to make," said Duncan. "It didn't take as long as we thought it might."

Garrido made a tent out of his fingers and peeped over the top of it. "A report has just been received from the Peninsular Hotel, a complaint that one of their guests has been molested."

"Well, there's a thing!" said Duncan. He picked up the electric razor on the desk, shook out the stubble and started to use it.

"This might be of interest to you," said Garrido.

The Canadian read the sheet of typescript and gave it to Raven. The letter was typed on the stationery of the Clínica Galvez.

OFFICE OF ALVARO MONTEIRO
PSYCHIATRIC DEPARTMENT
Ilona Maria Szechenyi

This patient was admitted on September 4, 1976, suffering from incipient schizophrenia. Examination indicated an abnormal emotional reaction coupled with impairment of judgment and thinking. Subject betrayed a high level of anxiety together with a reserved nature and sensitive personality.

There were no overt delusions but some denial of defence-mechanism. Subject's physical health was excellent. Her intelligence quotient was 140 on the Rorschach Scale.

Treatment was terminated when patient removed herself from the clinic October 8, 1976.

"Is it all right if I borrow this for a while?" asked Duncan.

"It is *not* all right," said Garrido. "You will find a photocopying machine at the end of the corridor. Room twelve. There is nobody there."

"I am glad to have this opportunity of talking to you privately," he said when the door had closed on the Canadian. "The police from Madrid have been on the phone. A Captain Alatren. He talked to my secretary. He would like to see you."

Raven's lips were suddenly dry. "Am I under arrest again, is that what you're saying?"

Garrido shook his head. "They have made no official request for you to be detained. If you want to take the first plane back to England, there is nothing that I can do to prevent it."

Raven took a long, deep breath. "And that's what you want me to do?"

"I will be frank with you," said Garrido. "For me you are a time bomb that will tick for as long as you remain in Portugal. My report will be at the Ministry of Justice at ten o'clock tomorrow morning. The Szechenyis were Spaniards, remember. That is why Madrid was informed. The minister may require me to make further inquiries. I cannot make them if you are not here."

The Canadian came through the door, brandishing the

Xerox. He returned the original. "An unexpected bonus. Thanks a lot, Rui."

He turned to Raven. "He's a busy man and it's Sunday. Let's you and I get the hell out of here."

The two men walked out into sunshine. The sound of a tug hooting cut through the chanting from the church.

"Tell her I want the lot," said Raven suddenly, nodding at the flower-seller. He pushed some bills into the woman's hand and loaded the baskets into the Porsche.

"Can we really trust him?" asked Raven, once he was seated.

"You're on the street, aren't you?" said Duncan. "He's a weird guy in many ways, but you can bank his promises."

"I'm taking the first plane out," said Raven.

"And your wife and Patrick?"

"The first plane out once they're here."

Duncan swivelled the rear-view mirror, inspecting a nick on his chin. "I don't think he liked me using his razor too much. An odd bugger. He's given me a head start. You'll see no official statement until tomorrow. Rui gets the glory but I get the audience. Let's go home and have breakfast."

The street door opened before he could use his key. Gaby Duncan was wearing a polka-dotted shirt and tight trousers. She held her husband close and looked over his shoulder at Raven.

"Everything's OK," said Duncan. "I'll tell you while John takes a bath."

He showed Raven into an old-fashioned bathroom with a mahogany-sheathed tub and wide-mouthed taps. Greenery grew in containers. Duncan opened a cupboard and spread a bath-sheet on the wicker armchair. He fetched Raven's bags from a neighbouring room.

"I guess you'll want to change. Help yourself to anything you need." He paused for a moment, looking down into the garden. "Lie if you want to keep her," he said, swinging round. "What the hell, just a passing urge of a sexual nature! You don't risk a marriage for that. Women don't *want* to know the truth, believe me!" He closed the door behind him.

Raven sank gingerly into the steaming water, the heat finding the points of pain and soothing them. He closed his eyes, thinking of what the Canadian had said. Kirstie and he were more than just lovers, they were comrades. Comradeship would last when love had gone, and it was that he could never betray. He wrapped himself in the bath-sheet and shaved.

He dressed in clean jeans and a shirt and put on a pair of loafers. The baskets of flowers he had bought were arranged in the sitting-room. Duncan and his wife were in the garden. A table was set for breakfast under the mulberry-tree.

Raven stepped cautiously over the terrier. "No food, just coffee, please!"

His hostess smiled at him. "You are feeling better?"

"A lot better, thanks." The idea that she knew about his affair with Ilona was a source of embarrassment to him.

"Gaby wants to come to the airport with us," said Duncan. He had changed into blues, an old faded slack suit.

"You won't mind?" said Gaby, pouring Raven's coffee.

"Of course not," he said.

Duncan lit a cheroot and exhaled luxuriously. "I just talked to the duty editor in Toronto. They want copy and photographs as soon as possible." They carried the breakfast things into the house, leaving the dog in the shade of the mulberry-tree. Raven threw his bags in the back of the Porsche and scrambled in after them.

Duncan started the motor and found a programme of jazz on the radio.

CHAPTER 11

Nobody spoke on the way to the airport. There was plenty of room to park. Duncan found a space outside the Main Terminal Hall. Beyond the fence, a mechanic in TAP blues wearing ear-protectors was guiding an airplane into its berth. Buildings and tarmac shimmered in a haze of heat. An empty baggage trolley stood on the steps near the entrance. Raven climbed out of the car and claimed it. He loaded his bags and slung his jacket on top of them.

"I'll see you people inside," he said.

Duncan leaned out over the top of his door. "What's that supposed to mean? Where are you going?"

Raven hesitated. A plane was circling above the wide river prior to making its descent. Another half-hour and the passengers would be coming out of the Customs Hall. It was difficult to explain how he felt.

Gaby let him off the hook, turning on her husband, her voice tart: "That's none of your business, Cam. We'll see you inside," she said to Raven.

Raven pushed the baggage trolley through the glass doors. Sunday sightseers had taken over the concourse, the bars and the restaurants. Others thronged the gallery, goggling at the planes screaming on the runways. Those booked on the planes were less exuberant, tending to stand in groups, surrounded by their possessions. Raven wheeled the trolley towards the TAP desk. He was half-way there when he saw the two men standing with their backs to the wall near the news-stand, hard-eyed men dressed in nondescript clothing whose heads moved in unison. One of them was the driver of the police car that had been parked near the Peninsular Hotel.

Raven leaned over the counter. "Do you speak English?"

The man nodded pleasantly. "Yes, sir, I do. May I help you?"

"The flight from London?"

The TAP clerk nodded at the Arrival Board. "Just landed, sir. Passengers will be coming through very shortly."

Raven steadied his voice. The two men were looking in his direction. "When does it take off again?"

"At seventeen hours, five o'clock."

Raven bent lower, displaying his passport and ticket. "I can't wait that long. Isn't there any other way of getting back to London before then?"

The clerk shook his head. "Not with us, there isn't. I know that the flight from Faro is booked solid, that's if you could get there in time. I had an inquiry only half an hour ago."

Duncan and Gaby were across the concourse drinking coffee at the bar. "How about if I changed planes?" asked Raven.

The clerk ran a finger down his flight schedule. He came to a stop and looked up. "There's a Sabena flight at noon. You could get a connection there to London. Do you want me to see if there's space?"

Raven nodded. "I need three seats."

The clerk pressed the keys on his computer and looked at the result on the screen.

"Tourist Class is completely full. It's Sunday, remember. I can give you three seats, but they would have to be First Class. It's an expensive way of getting back."

"I'll take the three," Raven said quickly. "The name is Raven. Mr. and Mrs. Raven and Mr. O'Callaghan."

The clerk indicated the cashier's office. By the time Raven had used his credit card, the tickets had been processed. Raven pushed the trolley across to the Duncans.

"Those men by the news-stand," said Raven. "Two of

them, standing together. The tall one's the driver of that police car."

Duncan's glance was casual. "You're making waves for yourself. I'd be surprised if those guys even know who you are. And if they did, all they'd want would be to see the back of you. I've already told you, Garrido doesn't give too much away, but you can bank any promise he makes."

Raven showed them the tickets. "If the worst comes to the worst and we can't make connection, there's always the train and the ferry. Anything to get the hell out of here." His voice sounded strained and anxious. The first passengers from London were coming down the aisle. Gaby touched Raven's sleeve. "It won't be as bad as you think," she said softly. "You'll see."

Raven put the tickets back in his pocket. "You people have been very good to me. I'm going to ask you one more favour."

"Shoot," said Duncan. All three of them were watching the door to the Customs Hall.

"I want to be alone with Kirstie. Just a few minutes. There are things that have to be said."

Duncan grinned over his wife's shoulder, holding her from behind. "You'd better get your act together. Here they come now!"

Raven pushed the trolley in Duncan's direction and made his way through the crowd. The disembarking passengers were coming towards him, blinking in the strong light as they searched for a familiar face. Kirstie and O'Callaghan were walking close together, Kirstie in a tight white skirt, blue top and white sling-back Guccis. She was taller by an inch than the lawyer, who was wearing a rose in his alpaca jacket.

Raven swallowed hard. "Over here!" he shouted.

The couple swung sideways, looking at Raven wide-eyed. Raven grabbed Kirstie quickly, burying his nose and mouth in her hair. He felt her body stiffen in his embrace. People were pressing from behind. O'Callaghan moved to let them pass.

"You bastard!" the lawyer said feelingly. The relief in his eyes belied his hostility. Kirstie wriggled out of Raven's grasp and smoothed her hair.

"Talk to Duncan," Raven said to the lawyer. "He'll tell you what's happened. They're over there!" He pointed across the hall.

O'Callaghan nodded, flashing a warning look before he moved off. Raven picked up Kirstie's travel-bag, gesturing at a vacant bench nearby.

"We need to talk."

He attempted to take her hand as they walked but she avoided it. He pulled her down on the bench beside him. O'Callaghan and the Duncans were over at the bar. Kirstie lit a cigarette, her movements swift and decisive, a sure sign of her anger. Her eyes hovered and held.

"I thought you had something to say."

He drew breath hopelessly. It was going to be worse than he had feared. "I'm not good at this and you know it. I'm sorry."

She tilted her head, her dark blue eyes cool. "You're going to have to do a lot better than that."

"Kirstie!" he pleaded. "Don't make it impossible for me. Things are bad enough as they are."

She moved to open attack, her nose thin, her face blanched under the sun-tan. "What are you trying to do to me, John? Am I supposed to be jumping with joy at the hero's return, is that it?"

"You're not being fair," he said, shaking his head.

"Fair?" She aimed the word at him like a bullet. "How I've lived with you for three years, I'll never know! I've been put in a police cell. My home has been invaded by criminals. This mania of yours for cheap glory has kept me in fear of my life. And you talk about being fair! You're insane, that's what you are. I don't know why the hell I married you."

"But you did," he said bitterly. "We had something going that would last forever. Your words, not mine, remember. Listen to me, please, Kirstie. Whatever happened between Ilona and me meant nothing. Nothing at all."

She blew a stream of smoke, her eyes still furious. "Maybe not to you."

"Something that's easily forgotten," he insisted doggedly.

"That's very bad thinking," she said. "It may be easy for you to forget. I find it more difficult."

He took her hand before she could stop him. "Is that all that this ring means to you? One mistake and my neck's on the block?"

"You're hurting me," she said quietly. He let her go. She dropped her cigarette butt on the ground and put her heel on it. Her eyes softened as she looked at him. "Patrick was right. You *are* a bastard. Was she better than me in bed? How was it?"

"You're the woman I love," he said. "I'd sooner lose my head than lose you. I've said that I'm sorry. I'm not going to grovel."

"I'm glad about that," she said. "It wouldn't suit you. No, it's hard and it's cruel, but I guess it's still a man's world. Just one thing. There won't be another time, remember."

He took both her hands, making her look at him full in the face. She smiled ruefully, for the past or the future, it was hard to know which.

"There won't *be* a next time," he promised.

A voice sounded in the speakers. "This is a call for passengers travelling on Sabena Flight. Three Forty-two to Brussels. Will passengers holding blue boarding-cards please go to Gate Seven for passport and customs control, passengers holding *blue* boarding-cards, please!"

"That's us," said Raven. Duncan was jumping up and down, pointing towards the departure gates.

N43

Kirstie dipped into her handbag and gave him an envelope. "I found this in the mailbox this morning!" It was addressed to him and blocked out in felt-penned printing.

ASK YOUR WIFE WHERE SHE SLEPT LAST NIGHT

He felt the colour leaving his face. She rose like a girl at her first dance. When he looked at her again, she was smiling.

"You already knew," he challenged. "You knew I'd been freed."

"I did," she admitted. "But that note might just have been true!"

She walked beside him lightly, the smile still on her face. The pressure of her hand on his arm was good to feel.

Donald MacKenzie is a successful Canadian writer who lives in Britain. He is the author of thirty novels of mystery and suspense published here and abroad. *Raven's Longest Night* is his first novel for the Crime Club.